## Praise for *Altered Heart*

"*Altered Heart* by Kate Steele is a spicy little appetizer sure to please even the most discerning reader's palate. This one is sure to leave her diehard fans in ecstasy and make first-time-Kate-Steele-readers into true believers."

-- Keely Stillman, *Ecataromance*

"*Altered Heart* is a wonderful story about werewolves and the power of love. I was captured by this story from the very beginning, and enjoyed following the characters as they struggled to accept their feelings."

-- Emily, Rainbow Reviews

"*Altered Heart* is an emotionally gripping, well written plot with realistic circumstances that most people can relate to. The real life characters lured me into the saga and held me spellbound to the very end of this tantalizing, thought provoking and very sensual tale. *Altered Heart* is a keeper to be read more than once."

-- *Literary Nymphs Reviews*

"This is a fabulous story and I wish that it could have gone on and on."

-- Hayley, *Fallen Angels*

# Loose Id®

ISBN 10: 1-59632-857-6
ISBN 13: 978-1-59632-857-0
ALTERED HEART
Copyright © January 2009 by Kate Steele
Originally released in e-book format in October 2008

Cover Illustration by Frauke Spanuth
Cover Design by April Martinez

**DISCLAIMER:** Many of the acts described in our BDSM/fetish titles can be dangerous. Please do not try any new sexual practice, whether it be fire, rope, or whip play, without the guidance of an experienced practitioner. Neither Loose Id nor its authors will be responsible for any loss, harm, injury or death resulting from use of the information contained in any of its titles.

Printed in the U.S.A. by
Lightning Source, Inc.
1246 Heil Quaker Blvd
La Vergne TN 37086
www.lightningsource.com

# ALTERED HEART

## Kate Steele

# Chapter One

Opening his eyes, Rio let his gaze focus on the pale, luminous orb of the moon. It was full tonight. That explained the increased tension on the street, the edgier, almost frantic mood that stalked the darkness. Whether others believed it or not, Rio was sure the full moon could affect some people. Emotions rose higher and hotter and faster. It could become a night of unsurpassed passion or pure, unmitigated disaster. All the possibilities in the world could line up and be subject to the desires and daring of each individual.

Gaze lowering, he noted the passing people. There were a few glances sent his way, but no one stopped. Not surprising. Everyone followed the unspoken cardinal rule that governed behavior on the street. Never stick your nose into someone else's business -- even if they looked like they needed help. Don't get involved. Don't step voluntarily into anything that had the potential to become unpleasant. He was glad no one stopped. The last thing he needed now was some well-meaning sap trying to help him out. Strangely cheered by that thought, he pushed away from the wall and turned to continue his way home when a large hand curled around his biceps, halting his progress.

"Hey, pretty boy. You looking for a date?"

Rio twisted his head and fixed his gaze on the man who spoke. He was tall, with shaggy brown hair and shadowed eyes, handsome in a rough, almost brutish way. He shifted his stance, and light from the blinking neon of a nearby bar whisked the shadows away. His eyes shone, no, glittered with some need, one that made Rio's senses tingle in alarm.

"Sorry. I'm through for the night," he said.

"That's too bad. I could make it well worth your while." The man pulled his hand out of his pocket to reveal a thick wad of cash. "Three hundred for your ass and half an hour of your time. What say, pretty?"

Rio eyed the cash and considered the offer. He could definitely use the extra money. Rent was coming due, not to mention he could go for a really good meal. Ramen noodles and peanut butter sandwiches were getting old despite the fact that he actually liked them. A steak would be a welcome change of pace.

"I don't do bareback," Rio warned, deciding to take a chance. "And I don't suck raw cock or swallow."

"Not a problem," the man agreed.

"You got a place?"

"Follow me."

Squelching his misgivings, Rio followed the stranger. He was broad shouldered and brawny. No one would dare shout "fag" at this guy. As they walked, a familiar sensation overtook Rio. He became calm, dispassionate, and uncaring, locking himself and his emotions away. It was a defense mechanism he'd cultivated to help him cope with the harsh realities of his life. Selling himself to strangers, letting them use his body for money was about as harsh as it got, but he had no choice.

A runaway at sixteen, he'd never finished high school and had no plans to do so. When he thought about it, one question came to mind: what use would a diploma be, anyway? It wasn't as though he'd ever be able to afford to go to college. Without any special skills or education, he couldn't find a job that paid more than minimum wage. Flipping burgers under the golden arches wouldn't pay his rent, let alone provide him with food and other necessities.

Two streets over, a familiar sight came into view. It was Sander's, a hotel that was a favorite haunt for those needing a room by the hour. A slight wave of relief calmed the small bit of tension he had yet to get under control. This was a known entity. He'd been here before. At least the sheets on the bed would be clean. No matter the reason the rooms were rented, the owner actually gave a shit about his place and his reputation.

They turned in at the entrance and Rio waited silently by the elevator doors while the man negotiated the rental rate with the desk clerk. Keycard in hand, he joined Rio and the two of them took the elevator to the third floor. The room numbers slid by as they walked the silent hall, then stopped before 308. After inserting the keycard, a flash of green indicated the lock had opened. His customer opened the door. Resigned, Rio followed him inside.

It was a typical hotel room, bland, utilitarian, and in this case, just plain dreary. The walls were painted a color that might have once been cream but was now borderline gray. It gave the place a gloomy, closed-in feeling, reminiscent of being under an overcast sky. The bathroom was to the left by the front door. The fixtures were old-fashioned with the sink sporting a rust stain under the dripping faucet. Farther inside was a queen-size bed, covered by a navy blue comforter decorated with garish pink and yellow roses. There was also a prefab dresser and a table with two chairs pulled up to it.

There was nothing else to see, nor any reason to waste time. Rio wanted to move forward, do the deed, and be gone before his mind could start screaming at him to get out.

"Strip," the man growled as he began to peel out of his own clothes.

"My money?" Rio coolly inquired.

Impatiently pulling the money from his pocket, the man dropped the agreed-upon amount on the dresser in a flutter of fifties and twenties.

"Satisfied?"

Nodding, Rio averted his eyes and complied with his customer's initial demand. After toeing off his shoes, he dropped his jacket, T-shirt, jeans, and briefs on one of the chairs, then pulled off his socks and laid them over his shoes.

"Nice. Just like I pictured. I do like them slender and young. How old are you, kid?"

"Eighteen," Rio replied, and watched a frown furrow the skin between the man's eyes. His body was hard and muscled. A pelt of dark, wiry hair covered his chest and abs and arrowed down to his groin. Surrounded by a thick bush, his cock rose aggressively hard and ready.

"Older than I thought, but you're definitely my type. On the bed."

Rio reached into his jacket pocket and brought out a condom and a single-use packet of lube. "Remember I said no bareback."

"Yeah, yeah. Do as you're told. I'm paying you good money for this."

Gritting his teeth against the need to sneer at the man's impatience, Rio obeyed. He pulled the comforter out of the way and climbed on the bed. His customer walked to the bathroom and with the snap of the wall switch, turned on the light before turning the rest of the room lights off. Everything was in shadow and Rio took some small measure of comfort from it. At least he wouldn't have to perform like some actor with bright lights illuminating every minute detail of what was about to happen on this shabby, sheet-covered stage.

"On your hands and knees," came the gruff order, and he submitted without demur.

When rough hands touched him, Rio kept his mind on the proceedings long enough to make sure the condom was used, then allowed himself to disappear. His cock remained in a semiflaccid state. There was no desire here, no need, no excitement. His body performed as expected and endured the rough fuck that followed. He absorbed the near-painful punishment meted out while his mind disconnected and engaged in a game of denial, distantly observing the act that finally came to a close. With a final hard thrust and grunt, the stranger filled the condom and withdrew.

Knees trembling, Rio collapsed on the bed. Breathing hard, he stared blankly at the whorls and patterns in the wood of the bedside table. When he felt his legs would hold him, he dragged himself from the bed. Donning his briefs, he gingerly took a seat on one of the chairs. He pulled his socks on; then, grabbing his jeans, he slid his feet into them. Standing, he pulled them up, fastened the button, and slid the zipper up. His client too had risen from the bed and walked toward the bathroom. Rio padded to the dresser and reached for the money.

"You were worth every penny."

Rio paused. Something was different. The man's voice had taken on a strange, harsh rasp. It grated over his nerves and sent a shard of alarm knifing into his gut.

"In fact, you were so good, I've decided to make you my new pet."

Gathering his courage, Rio answered, "Look, mister, I'm flattered, but I'm done here. All I want is the money you've already paid me."

"But there's so much more, pretty. So much more." The stranger reached out and turned off the bathroom light.

Darkness engulfed the room and panic roared to life within him. Rio froze, his limbs locked, unable to move. A rumbling growl permeated the stark silence. It sounded as though an angry dog had somehow gotten into the room. A cold sweat broke over his skin while prickles of terror stung like heated needles connecting with his nerve endings. Shocked into action, he backed away and stumbled woodenly against the chair he'd been sitting in. Rounding the table, he put it between him and the rest of the room. In the absolute pitch darkness he knew he didn't stand a chance of making it out. He needed light to find the door, light to make it past the madman who had him trapped.

Instinctively he reached for the curtains that covered the bank of windows that faced the street. He pulled them open. Looking back over his shoulder, his eyes widened at the sight of the glowing orbs and snarling face that appeared so unexpectedly close behind him. The terrified shout that ripped from his throat was abruptly silenced as he was violently thrown to the floor. The impact drove the breath from his body with a loud *whoosh*. Stunned, he wheezed in a hard-won gulp of air, but his attempt to recover was thwarted. His attacker straddled Rio's body, the man's weight pressing down hard and heavy. Hot breath branded his skin and obscenely wet licks against his shoulder and back made his flesh crawl.

"My pet," a hoarse, harsh voice declared before sharp teeth pierced the meat of his shoulder, penetrating so deep they scraped bone.

Rio's scream was muffled by a large, hard hand over his mouth. His body convulsively arched in shock. Pure agony exploded within him, driving every coherent thought away. He bucked and thrashed in vain, gasping when needle-sharp claws pierced his rib cage. Flesh parted and warm rivulets of fluid flowed beneath the fiery stings. Darkness, blacker than that of the room, filled his head and veiled his clouding vision. Rio shuddered and went boneless as consciousness blessedly deserted him. His compliant body was shaken, his flesh savaged, then released. Contented growls and wet laps of a busy tongue echoed in the silence of the room as the blood that freely flowed from his wounds was consumed with relish.

* * *

*One month later...*

From his seat at a table in the darkest corner of the room, Mick Matranga nursed a beer and waited. His target was slated to arrive any time now and he was impatient to get this over with. Not that it showed. Anyone looking at him, and many did, would see only a bland expression and relaxed movements.

Eyes the color of lush Kentucky bluegrass scanned the bar, approving the owner's use of vintage brewery memorabilia to give the place some added distinction. For the most part, the clientele seemed average. At least as average as one werewolf would appear to another. This bar was the favored hangout of the local pack and as such, few humans were allowed to patronize it. Those who dared cross the threshold were given a cold welcome and encouraged to go elsewhere.

As a stranger, Mick was given hostile looks by some of the locals, but as yet, none had dared challenge him. Apparently six feet four inches of height in combination with two hundred and twenty pounds of hard muscles were enough to keep anyone from acting foolishly territorial. A good thing too...for them. There was only one fight he was interested in tonight. Not that he'd turn any action down. That was, after all, why the committee had chosen him for this assignment. When it came to fulfilling his appointed tasks, he didn't hesitate if a recalcitrant subject resorted to violence. Mick would meet it head-on.

"Mark my words," Tuttle, the troll representative to the Committee for Supernatural Behavioral Enforcement, had once warned after a particularly nasty fight that concluded one of his assignments. "You'll meet someone tougher than you one of these days. You'd do well to cultivate a little diplomacy, Mick, if for no other reason than to save yourself a few bruises. Talking can do wonders. You know how to talk, right? You use your mouth and tongue for it."

Mick had given the disparaging troll a sour look before expressing his own opinion on the subject. "I have one thing to say to that. Giving someone a licking with my fists, rather than verbally sparring with mouth and tongue, is a far more satisfying expression of my feelings when they're pissing me off. I *am* an enforcer, after all. Bruises heal, Tuttle, and sometimes far quicker than the damage done by words. I'll leave those slippery things to you and the other committee members."

Mick snorted softly at the memory and took a sip of beer from his glass. He swallowed just as a stir at the front door drew his attention. A man strolled in and Mick dispassionately took his measure. He was big, with a wrestler's overly pumped physique, which may have accounted for the confidence that rolled off him in waves. His features held a slightly cruel cast, a twist of his lip revealing his contempt for the people who made way for him as he walked farther into the room. This had to be Kevin Sutter, alpha of the pack that used this bar as a gathering place. Dismissing him for the moment, Mick turned his attention to the person who was literally at Sutter's heel.

On hands and knees, head down with his shaggy, platinum-colored hair shielding his face, a slim boy crawled behind the imposing man. He was led by a silver chain-link leash, one that fastened to the tight leather collar around his neck. His clothes were filthy and there were bruises both fresh and fading on his arms where his shabby T-shirt left them bare. Scenting the air, Mick could smell a combination of stale sweat, semen, and fresh blood coming from him. The source of the blood became apparent as he moved. Rusty red trails came from his hands and knees as he followed in the wake of his "master."

Countenance revealing nothing, Mick steeled himself against the surge of utter contempt and fury that threatened to pull his wolf from his control. The wild, untamed creature inside him that was such vital a part of his psyche raged at this cruel treatment of one of his own. Young ones were to be protected, not abused. This wasn't one wolf dispatching another in honorable combat or demonstrating his dominance in an accepted and expected manner. This was blatant humiliation heaped on one of his kind and it shamed every werewolf in the room.

As he watched, Sutter took a seat at a booth and two other men joined him. The boy settled on his knees at Sutter's feet, his bleeding hands at rest in his lap. Without having to wait or ask, a pitcher of beer and glasses were immediately brought to them. The boy, with small, unobtrusive movements, picked at his hand and Mick saw a sliver of light flash from the bit of glass he pulled from his flesh before it hit the floor. Alerted by a slight change in the boy's posture, Sutter turned his attention to his slave.

"Did I say you could move?"

"No, sir," came the boy's immediate response. His tone was even, the words wooden and holding no inflection.

"You want your hands clean? Hold 'em out."

With just the slightest hint of hesitation, the boy did as he was told. Sutter picked up his glass and upended a splash of beer into his tormented charge's palms. Hissing at the sting of alcohol against raw, bleeding flesh, the boy curled his hands and brought them against his chest. His head bowed and his body quivered, but he said nothing, did nothing merely cradle his hands close, seeking to protect them from further abuse. Sutter laughed. The two men with him did as well, but even Mick could hear that the laughter was forced. He could see the underlying disapproval in their eyes.

The tension in the bar that had gathered when Sutter arrived grew until it became near stifling. It filled the room until the very air seemed to quiver. Mick could see more than one person aiming an almost imperceptible glance toward the front door. It seemed many longed to leave, but none dared. It was just as he'd been told; the entire pack was under Sutter's sadistic control and not one of them would publicly dare to stand up to him. But it hadn't prevented the anonymous reports about him being sent to the committee.

Mick felt his body gearing up for the coming confrontation. Sutter had to be taken down and no way in hell was he going to go peacefully. He obviously took great pleasure in terrorizing those weaker than himself, and what better situation could he find than this in which to indulge his vicious whims. He wouldn't give it up without a fight; Mick was willing to bet his life on that.

He once more took Sutter's measure. He was big, obviously strong and confident. He was also a bully, and bullies rarely challenged anyone they weren't sure they'd win against, which meant Sutter most likely hadn't faced a truly skilled opponent in ages, if ever. A challenge to his authority would make him lose his temper, and a man consumed by anger made mistakes. Tuttle's diplomatic advice be damned. Mick wasn't about to pull his punches with Sutter -- even if he had to deliberately provoke a violent reaction from the son of a bitch in order to neutralize him.

His own pack couldn't oppose him, but Mick certainly could and, in this case, he deemed it a pleasure. He casually rose from his chair, threw money on the table, and pulled an official-looking document from an inner pocket of his leather jacket. With a slow, measured stride he came abreast of Sutter's table and took a dominant stance over the three men seated there by looming over them. In combination with his obvious disregard for Sutter's alpha status and the steely, unwavering stare he cast upon him, it was a psychological move designed to intimidate. Mick casually threw the paper on the table.

A collective gasp sighed through the room and for a split second everyone froze.

With studied insolence, Sutter turned his attention to Mick. "What's this?"

"Kevin Sutter, this is a warrant issued by the CFSBE. You've been accused of various crimes under Section A7 of the Interspecies Behavioral Charter. As a duly appointed representative of the committee, I've been authorized to escort you to a formal hearing where you will be allowed to answers these charges. If you'll come with me, I have transport waiting for you outside." Mick paused for a moment. Sutter's beefy fist, wrapped around a mug of beer, tightened, his fingers flexing. Noting the man's reaction, Mick continued in a hard, no-nonsense tone. "And just for the record, failure to comply has you automatically declared a rogue and subject to being hunted by any CFSBE enforcer, of which I am one. I can take you in dead or alive, and I don't particularly care how you go. But go you will."

When Mick finished speaking, Sutter went completely still. The eyes of the men across from him widened and a split second later a rumbling growl issued from the depths of Sutter's chest. Like a demented fury, he sprang from his seat. His abrupt charge sent the boy at his feet sprawling across the floor. His reaction lightning quick, Mick dodged Sutter's attack as a tingling wave of energy swept across his acute senses. Sutter was changing and Mick wasted no time affecting his own shift.

Within the passing of a few swift seconds, two wolves, both deadly -- one enraged and one calmly assessing -- faced each other. Sutter's pack scrambled as far as possible out of the way, and with their backs to the walls, formed a loose circle around the combatants. With a vicious baring of teeth and a rough, threatening snarl, Sutter lunged at Mick. A nimble shift of his body took Mick out of harm's way, and he pivoted, his jaws closing on Sutter's flank. The thick pelt of Sutter's fur was little protection against the sharp teeth that tore into his flesh. Sutter howled and whirled, teeth snapping impotently on thin air as Mick spun out of reach.

A lethal dance ensued, both wolves circling as they looked for an opening, a vulnerability to attack. Sutter charged in several times, apparently believing brute strength alone would be enough to take his enemy down, but Mick patiently avoided those barreling rushes. He twisted and darted in, inflicting damage with each pass of their bodies. Sutter's blood and saliva joined the beer that spattered the floor under their feet. The man had gone completely feral, insanity shining in the glowing orbs of his eyes. Another charge sent him straight at Mick.

Prepared to dodge, Mick slipped in the slick combination of fluids under his feet. With a triumphant howl, Sutter slammed into him and both wolves went down in a tangle of flailing limbs and snapping jaws. A savage battle erupted with raking claws and tearing teeth the weapons of choice. Fur, blood, and spittle flew from the furious and brutal collision of those two lethal bodies, and tables and chairs were overturned in the wake of their cyclonic clash. So closely were they bonded in their struggle it was impossible to separate one from the other. They wheeled and rolled, regaining and losing their footing a dozen times over, tangling and fighting from one end of the room to the other. Their momentum sent them slamming against the base of the bar, the impact finally separating them. Both scrambled up and away. Panting and growling, they put some distance between themselves.

Mick's blood joined Sutter's on the floor. It dripped from a jagged slash along his ribs and several other shallow bites and claw slashes. Sutter was in even less pristine condition. A determined trickle of blood flowed from the wound on his flank and numerous other injuries added up to precious fluid loss that would steadily drain his strength. His head hung down, though his eyes remained fixed on Mick. His pants for air were harshly audible. Less winded, but hardly untaxed, Mick took the opportunity to breathe and evaluate his opponent's condition. It looked as though Sutter was reaching the end of his strength, and for a moment Mick almost believed he was ready to give up the fight. Almost. Between one second and the next, Sutter's exhaustion seemed to disappear. Emitting a near-maniacal, ululating howl, he rushed forward with a burst of unprecedented speed.

Far from being taken unaware, Mick was ready. Feinting with an aborted lunge of his body to the left, he triumphantly watched Sutter adjust his attack to follow, then with a twist of his head, Mick struck. His teeth sank deep into Sutter's overextended and unprotected throat. A burst of blood bathed his tongue, hot and copper rich. Sutter's agonized yelp was abruptly cut off, his windpipe crushed. Mick felt the flesh tear from his adversary's neck, and he braced himself against the hard yank of Sutter's body as its momentum carried him forward. The stunned, mortally wounded wolf stumbled and went down, his body hitting the floor with a hollow thud that spoke of utter defeat. Mercifully, Mick retained his hold. Rather than leave Sutter to suffer a nightmarish struggle for air and wheeze out his final breaths for endless, painful moments, Mick's actions swiftly cut what little flow was left to his opponent's lungs until the final beats of Sutter's heart played themselves out and stilled.

Releasing his hold on Sutter's torn throat, Mick stepped away. A chorus of howls rose and echoed through the room, causing his fur to bristle. Shudders ran under his skin, and he raised his head and joined in that wild and mournful chorus. As their tribute to the dead faded away, Mick transformed.

His clothes were ripped and bloodstained. He winced at the touch of cloth against the wound on his ribs and eased out of his shredded jacket and T-shirt, laying them on the bar. The steady drip of blood from his injury slowed and stopped. Ripped and jagged flesh began to seal itself until nothing remained but a slightly irregular line of flesh that showed pink against his tan.

He raised his gaze from the healed wound and looked around him. Excitement and stress had caused some of those present to shift. A half dozen wolves mingled uneasily among the still human-shaped members of Sutter's pack. Human and wolf alike watched him expectantly, and Mick felt his cock stir. He could take them. He *had* defeated their alpha. He could take this pack and make it his own. A part of him, the base instincts driven by his wolf, cried out that he do just that, but the human side of him quickly won out. He'd never wanted to lead a pack, and he wasn't about to do so now. He was going to finish what he'd been sent here to do, but the temptation, the gut-deep natural impulse to claim his alpha's due left him aroused and edgy.

Those feelings colored his voice and the harsh accusation he threw at those assembled. "With the help of an informant, a body was discovered on Kevin Sutter's land. It was the body of a young man. One of the committee's associate witches cast a reconstruction spell over it so we could learn the identity of the deceased and what happened to him. His name was Daniel Taylor and he was sixteen years old. He was turned by Sutter, raped, beaten, humiliated, and murdered. Sutter would have stood before the CFSBE to answer for his crimes but you, all of you, will face no such charges even though you did nothing to help that boy."

A stunned and guilty silence filled the room. The stillness was absolute until one man stepped forward. He was one of the two who'd arrived with Sutter. "You're right. We did nothing, and we all share in that shame. Our only excuse is that *he* was our alpha." A jerk of his head indicated the man lying dead on the floor. In death, Sutter had regained his human body. "The alpha is the head and heart of the pack. How can the body do what's right when the head and heart that rule it are defective but too powerful to defeat?"

Grudgingly Mick considered his words and nodded. What the man said was true; an alpha held the lives of his pack in his hands. He had power over them that went far beyond simple leadership. He could control each individual with his strength, fighting prowess and sometimes, in the case of the weaker members, by his will alone. It was a responsibility not to be taken lightly. To guide a disparate group of individuals whose one link was the fact that they were werewolves, to hold them together, to see the pack prosper as a whole was not an easy task. The pack should be a haven that offered companionship and security despite the occasional fights that accompanied the inevitable jockeying for position within the hierarchy. Kevin Sutter had betrayed his pack, terrorized them, and brought them misery, and yet his strength kept them under his rule and trapped by his twisted psyche.

His gaze met that of the man who'd addressed him. "Now's your chance for change."

"Will you take his place?"

Mick shook his head though once again his inner wolf railed at him while his body tensed in protest. His cock throbbed with the need to fuck, to plant his seed as an affirmation of having survived a battle that could have cost him his life. "Not my thing. I came here with a job to do."

He dismissed the question of pack leadership and his own desires by searching the room for the one other detail that required his immediate attention. Under the table at the booth where Sutter had sat when he first entered the bar, a frail body cowered. Mick approached the boy and squatted down. "Kid, you can come out now. Nobody's going to hurt you."

With his face turned to the wall, the boy at first remained exactly where he was. His knees were pulled up, his head tucked against them with his arms wrapped tightly around his shaking body. Mick could smell the fear rolling off him and was just about certain he was going to have to physically pull the kid out from his hiding place until a slight movement proved him wrong. Slowly, the young man's defensive posture eased. His chin came up and he turned his head.

Mick quickly stifled his indrawn breath of surprise. The boy's countenance was, quite simply, angelic. Though overly thin, his oval face was the perfect frame for a pair of tender, lush, and faintly rose-tinged lips and the slim, straight nose that rose over them. His pale, fine and creamy skin nearly begged to be touched, but it was his eyes that truly mesmerized. Liquid silver-gray with a hint of midnight blue around the rim of the iris, they were large and luminous. Thick lashes and slightly winged brows emphasized their hypnotic beauty. Though tousled and dirty, his platinum hair still somehow managed to attract the light as though it couldn't bear the thought of leaving untouched that which so richly deserved to shine.

A renewed surge of pure lust assaulted Mick, but he fought it down. If his time with Sutter resembled Daniel Taylor's experiences, this boy had been through hell. He wasn't about to add to the kid's nightmares. Putting a lid on his physical response to the pup, Mick backed off a bit.

"Come on out now," he encouraged, frowning at the soft, husky rasp of his own voice. Apparently there were parts of himself that weren't going to be amenable to his will where it concerned his attraction to this young stranger. Casting off his annoyance, Mick waited.

The boy considered him for a moment then slowly wiggled from beneath the table. On legs that were a little unsteady he stood then reached up to the collar that encircled his throat. Trembling fingers unbuckled the thick leather strap attached to the dangling chain leash. Mick frowned at the sores beneath the collar but noted that the flesh began to heal almost immediately. Leather and metal dropped to the floor with a ringing thump. The kid's gaze traversed the floor and came to rest on the man who had tormented him for so long. His bare feet moved and with a few wobbly steps, he stood next to the body.

A harsh, anguished wail broke from the boy and before anyone could react he began kicking Sutter's supine body. "You bastard! You lousy, low-life, sadistic son of a bitch! I hate you! I hate you!" His screamed obscenities echoed off the walls and ceiling, his terror and loathing a living entity. Mick flinched and noticed a similar reaction from nearly every person present.

Mick was the first to break from the jarring shock caused by the boy's actions. He grabbed the kid from behind and wrapping his arms around that wiry torso, pulled him away from Sutter's body. "Whoa, now. Ease up, kid. He's dead. He can't hurt you anymore. You hear me? He can't hurt you anymore."

Seemingly caught up in a storm of out of control emotions, the boy struggled and fought like a wild thing caught in a trap. He snarled and screamed, his fingers curling into claws, his nails raking across Mick's arms. When he tried to bite as well, Mick had enough. He carefully tightened his grip, making it more and more difficult for the boy to breathe.

"Stop it. Stop it right now," Mick curtly ordered. His words and actions left no room for disobedience.

With his air supply dwindling, the distraught youngster began to whimper, his senses returning. Mick loosened his grip and the boy took a few deep breaths then collapsed against him. His rough, broken sobs accompanied shakes so deep Mick had reason to wonder why the kid's teeth weren't rattling. Any remaining lust he'd felt dissolved in a wave of baffled concern. At a total loss as to what to do, his wolf's instincts took command. Mick hoisted the young one up into his arms, found an upright chair among the tangled mess of furniture and sat down. Settling the distressed pup in his lap, he offered a throaty, crooning growl and rubbed the boy's back in an unpracticed but gentle manner. That slim body curled itself around Mick and he bent his head, nuzzling his cheek against the boy's hair.

"There now. Let it go. Just let it go, kid," Mick gruffly whispered.

Hot tears trickled down his chest from where the boy had laid his cheek against Mick and his warm, hiccupping breaths caressed Mick's bare skin. Though sorry for what caused the kid's tears, oddly enough he found himself liking the sensations they created. It felt intimate and satisfying to offer protection and comfort to the young one. It was too bad it had to be under such horrific circumstances.

Taking a deep breath, he let the boy's scent fill his nostrils. Beneath the myriad scents of dirt, sweat, fear, blood and tears, Mick noted something more. The underlying aroma was musky, with a mildly sweet tang that rose with the warmth of his body. It intrigued him and urged Mick to take stronger note of the young werewolf in his arms. He felt a stirring deep inside, an awareness that slowly bloomed beneath his puzzled consciousness. His mind teetered on the brink of acknowledging some snippet of information, some small fact of large import. The realization and understanding of what tickled his brain and senses was just within reach when it was suddenly dashed away by the sudden thrashing movements of the pup he held so close.

Hands planted themselves on his chest and an angry voice began demanding, "Let me go. Let go. Get your fucking hands off me!"

Irritated to have his thoughts interrupted, Mick's protective instincts evaporated and he promptly complied. The struggling boy tumbled out of his lap and hit the floor with a dull thump. He looked up at Mick with wide, accusing eyes.

Mick shrugged. "You said to let go, so I did."

"Bastard," the boy said, angrily spitting the word.

"Afraid not. My parents are actually married. The name's Mick Matranga, and who might you be?"

"None of your fucking business."

"I could go for the obvious joke and say that's a really odd name, but I think I'll pass and just say you're wrong about that. You're under my protection until the CFSBE figures out what to do with you. It would be convenient to have a name for you unless you're ready to settle for being called 'hey you.'"

A few muffled snickers followed Mick's comeback. A swift glance around reminded him of the presence of those who had witnessed Sutter's defeat. Their amusement was good to hear and helped alleviate the emotionally charged atmosphere from moments ago.

"I don't need your protection. You and your freaky organization can go to hell."

"You don't need help? Doesn't look like you were doing a bang-up job of helping yourself before I came along."

"I didn't ask for this. I didn't ask for that fucking sick psycho bastard to pick me up. I just want to go…" The boy hesitated as though unsure of just where it was he wanted to go.

"Where? Home?"

"Yeah."

The uncertainty in the boy's voice made Mick wonder if there was such a place for him. "Too bad. You're not going anywhere on your own."

"Why? Why can't you just leave me *alone*?!" The boy's strident yell had Mick gritting his teeth and reaching for his patience.

"If I turn you loose, you'll just get into more trouble. You're an untrained, unprotected pup, and until you learn a few things you're sticking with me. Got it?" Mick stood and towered over the young one.

Eyes filled with resentful fury followed the length of Mick's body and halted on his determined face. "You can't make me."

A confident and amused smile curved Mick's lips at that childish reply. "Can't make you? Listen carefully, kid. The job I was given entailed two things. Bring in Kevin Sutter dead or alive, and take charge of you. There's part one." He pointed to Sutter's body. "You're part two. You want to try me?"

Something in Mick's eyes must have convinced his new charge. The boy dropped his challenging gaze and muttered under his breath. Those barely audible curses made Mick grin. The kid had backbone. He'd give him that. Leaving the boy to his own devices for the moment, Mick crossed the room and grabbed up his T-shirt. Putting it on, he grimaced and skimmed the ripped and soiled fabric down his torso.

"Nothing like sweat and blood. Christ, I need a bath," he muttered, then looked around for the man he'd spoken to a few moments before. "You. Who's pack beta?" he asked, motioning the man over while he examined the ruins of his leather jacket.

"I am," the man answered.

Mick gave him a considering look, tossed his jacket back on the bar, then shrugged. "Clear this place out, will you? I think it's safe to assume business is over for the night." He glanced at the bartender who gravely nodded his agreement. "Oh, and uh, despite what I said, I don't really need to bring him in now." He nodded his head in the direction of Sutter's body. "I'm delegating disposal of the body to your pack. Do a good job of it."

"We'll take care of it. That, at least, we can do."

With a short nod, Mick turned to the bartender. "I could really use a beer."

The man snorted softly and smiled. He set Mick up with a foamy mug of draft and silently they watched the majority of the pack file out. Four men stayed and after a short conference, one left and reentered a moment later with a folded tarp in hand. Sutter's body was carefully wrapped and carried out. The bartender locked the door after them and returned to his place behind the bar.

Taking a deep breath, Mick let the tension slowly ease from his shoulders. With a glance toward the back of the bar he noted his charge had made himself comfortable in one of the booths. Back to the wall, knees pulled up and feet resting on the bench seat, he appeared to be dozing. With his eyes closed and his features relaxed he looked to be the epitome of innocence. Suddenly feeling old, weary, and a bit melancholy, Mick let his gaze linger for a moment on that beautiful face. Knowing that whatever naiveté the kid had once possessed was probably long gone increased Mick's gloomy mood. A kid that age should be in school, chasing girls, and raising just enough hell to keep things interesting.

With a slight shake of his head he turned back to the bartender. "So. Problem solved."

The man gravely nodded but said nothing. His expression was stoic, his dark eyes giving nothing away.

"You saved that kid's life."

"But not the first one. I should have contacted the CFSBE sooner," the bartender mournfully admitted. "I'll regret that for the rest of my life."

"Going against your alpha wasn't an easy thing to do."

"Just traitorous."

"No. Sutter was a sadistic bastard preying on those weaker than himself. What he was doing was clearly wrong and if you'd challenged him you'd have died and the boy with you. Then God knows how many others. You had the strength to do the right thing. Doing what's right, acting in good conscience doesn't make you a traitor." Mick stared at the man, willing him to believe the truth of his words.

The man finally nodded, and though glumly expressed, a bit of relief showed in his eyes. "Thanks. I'll take what comfort I can from that. So what now? What happens to *him?*" A slight jerk of his head indicated Sutter's former slave.

Mick sighed. "Depends. What can you tell me about him? Know his name?"

"Sutter mostly just referred to him as his pet, but I did hear him call the kid Rio a couple of times. Whether that was really his name or just something Sutter made up, I don't know."

"He always make him wear that collar and chain?"

"As far as I know. He was wearing it every time Sutter showed up here with him. Sutter was a mean son of a bitch. You saw for yourself. He abused the kid plenty, but the worst thing he did was to prevent him from changing."

*"What?"*

"The three nights of the last full moon," the man specified. "You know how it is for a human who's been turned. That first change is unstoppable. Or so I thought. You remember how excruciating it was the first time you shifted?"

"Like I'd ever forget." While time eased the remembered painful intensity of that first shift, he seriously doubted anyone could completely erase such an unpleasant memory.

"Sutter wouldn't let him change. He used his alpha's will to prevent it. He brought the boy in here and made us watch. The pup screamed and cried while his body practically tried to turn itself inside out." The bartender's eyes filled with a bleak horror. "I can still see it, the muscle and bone and flesh snapping and stretching and desperately reaching for the change. For three nights I watched that kid beg until he finally passed out from the pain while Sutter watched him like he was some kind of lab experiment. I'd never seen madness before, but it was there in Sutter's eyes. I couldn't let it go on anymore. I just couldn't."

His voice had gone shaky and the glitter of unshed tears sparkled in his eyes as he related the boy's torture. Mick lowered his gaze from the man's face, giving him a modicum of privacy to recover. He felt ill himself. Any regret he had at having killed Sutter was burned away. Whether it had been sickness or pure evil that caused him to do what he'd done, the world was a better place without him in it. Of that he was certain.

He glanced around the room, fully noting for the first time the damage that he and Sutter had wrought during their fight. Welcoming a way to change the subject, he drolly commented, "Damn. This place is trashed."

The bartender's short bark of laughter announced his recovery. "You think?"

Mick met his eyes and grinned. "My boss is going to love me. I'll help you file a claim with the CFSBE for the damages."

"Not necessary."

"Why?"

"Sutter's paying."

"How so?"

"As luck would have it, he doesn't have any family, which is probably a damn good thing. God knows what he would have done to them, but at any rate, that being the case, his property and anything of value he had is settled on the pack. I'll claim the damages out of the proceeds. With the entire pack here to bear witness as to what happened, there won't be any protest."

Mick nodded. "All right, but if for some reason it doesn't work out, contact me at the CFSBE offices. I'll be filing a report. It'll all be on record, including this," he said with a gesture that indicated the state of the room. Pulling his cell phone from an intact pocket of his battered jacket, Mick took a few pictures of the damage.

"Will do," the bartender agreed.

Folding his phone and putting it away, he downed the last of his beer and headed across the room to collect his new charge. The boy didn't stir or open his eyes, but Mick noted the slight tensing of his body that spoke volumes. He knew Mick was there. "Yo, kid, let's go."

"My name's not kid."

"So what is it?"

"Harry."

Mick's brow rose and a smile curled one corner of his mouth. "Try again and keep in mind, I can smell a lie…Rio."

The boy's eyes opened, those surprised yet speculating silver orbs landing on Mick in a way that turned his next heartbeat into an almost painful thud. Controlling his expression, Mick waited.

"Yeah, it's Rio."

"Rio what?"

"Hardin."

"How old are you?"

"Twenty-three." Mick's steady regard brought a scowl to Rio's face. "Jeez. Eighteen, all right?"

"Fine by me. Let's go." Mick turned his back and started walking. Behind him, he heard Rio scramble out of the booth.

"Where are we going?"

"Greenfield, Indiana."

"Why there?"

"'Cause that's where I live."

"You're taking me home with you?"

"For now until I get instructions from my boss on what to do with you."

"Fuck that."

Mick glanced back. Rio had halted his forward progress and stood with arms crossed over his chest. "What's the problem?"

"I just spent four weeks with one werewolf psycho who took me home with him. I'm not volunteering for another round."

"First of all, I'm not a psycho. I'm a duly appointed officer of the CFSBE. You have heard of it, right?"

With a grudging shrug of his shoulders, Rio nodded.

"Then you should know that being an enforcer for the CFSBE is like being an FBI agent, a cop, or any other law enforcement officer you can think of."

"That still doesn't mean I can trust you."

"No, I suppose it doesn't, but here's where you get lucky. I have bosses to answer to. You're a known entity to them.

You're part of my assignment. It's my job to take care of you. If I abuse you in any way all you have to do is report me."

"Sure. And they're gonna take my word over yours," Rio answered with a disdainful and disbelieving sneer.

"If you're telling the truth they will, and they have ways of knowing."

"Even that won't help me if you decide to get rid of me like you did that fucking son of a bitch bastard you just wasted."

"And why would I do that?"

When Rio didn't answer, Mick sighed in frustration and ran a hand through his already tousled dark hair. The fall of bangs he disturbed cascaded back over his forehead when he took his hand away. "Look, I know you've been through hell. All I can tell you is I'm here to try to make things better. I've got no plans to kill you, beat you, or whatever the hell else you think I might want to try with your scrawny ass. I'm tired. I'm filthy. I fucking stink, I'm starving and part of the reason I just killed a man was to get you free of him. The only thing I want to do right now is grab some food somewhere, go back to my motel, eat, shower and pass out for a few hours. You coming voluntarily, or do I have to cuff you and drag you with me?"

"Don't try to pretend you know what I've been through or that you did what you did for me," Rio snarled. A growl rumbled up from the depths of his chest and his eyes widened in surprised dismay.

Despite the pain and anger expressed in Rio's words, Mick struggled to hide the unexpected spurt of amusement the boy's expression caused. Rio was obviously not used to the way his newly developing inner wolf had suddenly chosen to express its distrust of the situation.

"I'm not trying to pretend anything," he answered in a matter-of-fact way he hoped would calm the boy. "I'm just making a general acknowledgment of what happened to you, pup. And yeah, my main objective was to make Sutter stand and answer for what he's done. But that doesn't change the fact that the result was getting you cut loose from him. The main point I'm trying to make at the moment is whatever the hell you've been through, wouldn't it be easier to face it on a full stomach? I'd be willing to bet you haven't had a decent meal in a while. Huh?"

Trying to curb his impatience, Mick waited. At the mention of food, he watched as Rio bit his bottom lip, worried it for a moment, then nodded.

"Come on then. Food, a hot shower, some uninterrupted sleep in a bed with clean sheets. Sounds good, doesn't it?" At Rio's immediate look of suspicion, Mick reassured him. "The room's got two beds. One of 'em's all yours. All right?"

At Rio's second nod, Mick sent the bartender, who'd been watching with amused interest, a nod and strode out the door. He crossed the gravel parking lot and keyed open the locks on his SUV with the remote. Looking back, he saw Rio carefully trying to pick his way barefoot across the sharp stones.

"Shit," Mick said, softly cursing at himself. He opened the passenger door and marched back to Rio. Without a word he swung the slim young man up in his arms.

Rio barely had time to utter a protesting, "Hey!" before he was deposited in the passenger seat.

"Buckle up," Mick tersely commanded before rounding the front of the vehicle to the other side. He levered himself behind the steering wheel, snapped his seat belt into place and started the engine. "Tomorrow we get you some clothes and shoes. I'll lend you a clean pair of sweats and a T-shirt for tonight. Drive-through all right with you? There's a roast beef place just up the street from the motel."

"Yeah. That's fine."

Mick glanced over at his passenger. Rio stared straight ahead, his eyes half lidded as though mesmerized by the scenery outside the window. Mick had a feeling the reality of the situation would be hitting before long. Having been freed of his tormentor, Rio's emotions were most likely in a state of flux. It would take him a while to level out, which was why Mick chose to overlook the tantrums and other recalcitrant behavior. The kid would be coming down with a thump, and most likely he'd bounce more than once.

## Chapter Two

From the bar's location at the edge of town, the drive to his motel took less than ten minutes. Mick bypassed the motel's driveway in favor of the fast food restaurant he'd mentioned to Rio. He ordered enough food to feed a small army then returned the way he'd come. He parked in the motel's lot and grabbed the bags of food. Rio helped by taking the tray holding their drinks, and Mick led the way to his room. A keycard opened the door, and Mick ushered Rio in ahead of him.

"Just set it down on the table. Bathroom's right there if you want to wash your hands before you eat," Mick said.

Rio followed his directions and Mick heard the water run in the sink while he tore open the food bags, using them as makeshift placemats. The smell of roast beef made his mouth water and his stomach rumble. Rio came out with a clean face and hands and took a seat. Mick took his turn in the bathroom and returned to find Rio waiting.

"Dig in. There's plenty."

Without saying a word, Rio opened a sandwich wrapper and, after a couple of careful bites of bread and warm meat, began to devour it as though he hadn't tasted food in weeks. Mick wasted no time emulating him. He nudged fries and a couple more of the sandwiches in Rio's direction as well as one of the extra-large cups of cola. The two of them ate without talking, the silence broken only by the sounds of chewing and paper rustling as more food was unwrapped and consumed. When the last bite was swallowed, Mick sat back with a satisfied sigh.

"Oh yeah. Now I feel more human."

Rio laughed, the sound holding a slight edge of hysteria. "Human? Not anymore. Never again."

*So it begins*, Mick thought. "No, never again. There's nothing that can change it now. I know you didn't ask for this, but it's not a bad thing to be. I think you'll come to find there are advantages to being a were."

"Such as?"

"Superior strength, healing power, immunity to disease. Letting your wolf free to run and hunt. It's a heady thing."

"Don't talk to me about that! I'm never going to change!"

Sympathy welled inside Mick at the absolute terror expressed in Rio's words. But he saw no use in trying to whitewash the situation. "Look, I know what he did to you. It was beyond cruel and believe me, I know how painful the first transformation can be. It's that way for all of us, but for Sutter to drag it out the way he did and not let you make the final shift…" Mick's fists clenched and he carefully reined in his growing fury at the thought. It wasn't going to help anything for both of them to be upset. He took a deep, calming breath. "I understand why you're scared, but that doesn't change the fact that when the next full moon comes around you *will* shift. At least this time there won't be anything to interfere and you'll have help to get through it. You're going to have to trust me on this."

"I don't trust anybody," Rio muttered, his expression sullen and shuttered.

"I get that." Mick rose and went to his duffel bag. He pulled out the clean clothes he'd promised Rio. "Here. Why don't you take a shower?"

Silently, Rio accepted what Mick offered and disappeared into the bathroom. When the shower started up, Mick pulled a laptop computer from its case and set it up on the bed. Taking a seat, he reached into his jacket pocket for his cell phone and hit a button to speed dial a number. His call was answered on the second ring.

"Hey there, handsome. What's up?"

Mick grinned at the familiar greeting. "I'd like to say nine inches, but I'm too damn tired for that."

A spate of female laughter sounded in his ear. "Are you bragging?"

"Just stating the facts, sweetheart."

"Ooo, I do like honesty in my men along with their other more sizeable assets. So what can I do for you this evening, sugar? Or did you just call to talk dirty to me? Not that I mind. Maybe a little phone sex would counter your exhaustion. Not too many people know this, but I've got experience under my belt in that arena."

A series of panting breaths and heartfelt moans drifted over the line and Mick laughed. "Shit, Galaviz, you keep that up and I'll forget why I called."

Graciella Galaviz was a sylph and the CFSBE's premier computer whiz and researcher. Though they seldom met in person, she and Mick had quickly developed an easy friendship. Galaviz was smart, sassy and the most compassionate being Mick had ever met. She genuinely loved her job for the role she was able to play in helping those in need, which completely countered the idea that sylphs were soulless creatures. For an air elemental, Galaviz had heart to spare and quicksilver fingers that could make a computer spit out information almost faster than it could be requested.

"Spoilsport. All right, I'll behave. So seriously, what can I do for you, Mick?"

"I need whatever information you can dig up on a kid by the name of Rio Hardin. He's eighteen, about five-nine, gray eyes, pale blond hair, slim build. I don't have anything more on him than that." Mick could hear the rapid tapping of keys on a keyboard.

"This definitely could be him. Rio James Hardin. There was a missing person's report made on him by the boy's father. It was filed two years ago in Pittsburgh. You got your laptop? I'll shoot this to you."

"Ready and waiting."

"On its way. Are you looking for this boy? He's a real cutie."

"Already got him."

"Is he all right? Bet his parents will be relieved."

"He's as fine as anyone who got turned into a werewolf by a nutcase can be. He's been through some bad shit."

"Oh, I'm so sorry to hear that. What are you going to do with him?"

"I've got to get instructions from Booth. He can't go home as is. He hasn't gone through his first transformation yet, which I doubt would go over well with the folks at home even if they could handle it. Not to mention that it looks as though he may be a runaway. Going home is probably the last thing he needs right now."

"Well, I'm sure you'll get things ironed out, Mick. Damn, I've got another call coming in. Hey, sexy man, you take care of yourself."

"You too, gorgeous."

"Flatterer."

Galaviz ended the call and Mick speed dialed a second number. Waiting for it to connect, he studied the information that came up on his laptop's screen. The picture on the missing person's report was indeed a younger version of the young man who was now showering in his bathroom. Rio's father, James R. Hardin, had reported the boy as missing a little over two years ago. Notes on the case file indicated that there had been no signs of drug abuse or gang activity. For all intents and purposes, he'd been a typical sixteen-year-old boy attending high school.

The investigating officer included interviews with the boy's friends and his school guidance counselor. His school records indicated that things had been fairly steady and mundane until the year Rio turned twelve, when his mother died. His grades had taken a nosedive for a while but had soon leveled out and returned to normal. Not long after his fourteenth birthday his records noted that Rio's father remarried. Several months after that, Rio's grades again took a header. According to the guidance counselor, though he customarily possessed a sunny disposition, Rio became sullen and uncommunicative. He even started skipping classes. Things remained that way until the boy disappeared.

While it wasn't noted on his records, the guidance counselor had informed the investigating officer that she suspected some kind of problem at home. There were no reports of incidents with other students or teachers. His mother's death had certainly affected Rio and while acquiring a stepmother had at first seemed to have little impact on him, certainly something had triggered this new disturbance in Rio's behavior. The only thing that seemed to have recently changed in the boy's life before the trouble began was this new addition to his family.

Mick was considering the reports when his call was answered. "Booth."

"Hey, boss," Mick responded.

"Mick. How'd it go?"

"Not as planned."

"Let me guess. The subject proved uncooperative."

"Big time."

"You take him down?"

"All the way. He wouldn't back off." Mick waited while his boss's sigh gusted over the phone line.

"This is getting to be a habit. There may be an inquiry."

"I stand by my actions. Sutter's pack will bear witness to what happened."

"Good, then there's no problem, but I want a full report on my desk when you get back."

"Will do. Listen, that was the good news."

"And the bad news?"

"It's the kid Sutter was holding. Name's Rio Hardin. He's eighteen. That crazy bastard took him to replace Danny Taylor, the boy he murdered. The new kid's been turned, but he's never shifted. I had Galaviz do a search on him and he was in the system as a missing person. Looks like he's a runaway. I've got him with me. The next question is, what do I do with him?"

"Under the circumstances it would hardly be advisable to turn him over to his family. He's eighteen, you say?"

"Yeah."

"Legally of age to be independent. I think we'll leave the decision as to whether he contacts his family up to him, but for now he needs to be placed with someone to teach him what it means to be a were. A pack would be the ideal situation for him. There's no way he can be on his own; he'd be eaten alive without someone to protect him. Let me make a few calls and I'll get back to you."

"All right."

Ending the call, Mick replaced his cell phone and laptop. The shower was still running. He stood and walked to the bathroom door. Standing completely still, he carefully listened. Beneath the fall of water he could hear muffled sobs and he felt a gut-deep twinge of sympathy. Once again he felt the impulse to protect and soothe this young one who'd been so traumatized. Trouble was, he was too late to protect

Rio. The damage had been done. Sympathy and compassion were all he could offer the boy now, and it left him feeling frustrated, angry, and more than a little bit confused as to why he wanted to do anything at all.

Mick was all about bringing in the bad guys and righting wrongs; it was the picking up of the pieces afterward that made him feel inadequate. Normally he didn't let that bother him. Those things weren't his province to deal with. There was nothing that could be said or done to change the bad things that people went through. They just had to live with it and cope. It didn't seem fair, but then, whoever said life was fair? He was used to doing his job and putting each case and the people involved behind him without qualm. What was it about this kid that was getting under his skin, and did it really matter? As soon as Booth found a place for him, Rio would no longer be his responsibility. That thought brought with it an odd pang of something strangely close to denial. For some reason, letting Rio go seemed…wrong.

Disturbed by this peculiar feeling, Mick chose to ignore it and wandered back to the bed closer to the room's outer door. He toed off his shoes, piled the pillows up and settled down with his back to the headboard. Grabbing the remote off the bedside table, he turned on the television and was idly flipping through the channels when Rio emerged from the bathroom. He was wearing the clothes Mick had loaned him and Mick found himself suppressing a smile. They were way too big, the effect that of a little kid wearing an adult's clothes to play dress-up. The hem of Mick's T-shirt fell to mid-thigh on Rio. He'd rolled the bottoms of the sweatpants legs to form cuffs and fortunately there was a drawstring in the waistband, which he was apparently able to tighten enough to keep them up.

His hair was sleek and clean and slightly fluffy from having the motel-provided blow dryer used on it. The pale strands shimmered even under the glow of artificial light. There was evidence left behind of Rio's tears, the slight swelling of his eyelids. His lips too were a bit swollen, and their intensified color made them seem even lusher than before. Mick wondered why crying would affect them like that. Not that it looked bad. In fact it made the kid just that much more tempting.

With his eyes on Rio, Mick calmly acknowledged to himself the fact that he was attracted to this young man. That in itself wasn't unusual or cause for distress. Mick had been sexually active with males and females alike. He generally had no preference when it came to one or the other. The few partners he had since the death of his wife four years earlier had been temporary, just warm bodies to slake his lust. While he'd liked everyone he'd been with, there'd been nothing special about his association with them.

But this kid's presence, for some reason, was pricking at the barriers Mick put up between himself and others. He wasn't happy with the emergence of long-repressed impulses and emotions, and he definitely didn't know what to do about them. Especially the guilt caused by lusting after someone so young.

Even at eighteen, Rio was barely more than a kid and one who'd just spent several weeks in the hands of an unbalanced sadist. There was no doubt in Mick's mind that sexual abuse had to have played a part in the torment Sutter had visited upon him. The last thing he needed was lust from the man who had rescued him. Mick knew that and yet his body kept quickening at the sight of Rio. His wolf was straining to be close to the kid in a way that had only happened once before. With his wife, his mate. Refusing to even think about what that meant, Mick settled for being annoyed.

Frowning, he levered himself up and off the bed. He rummaged in his duffel and gathered some clean clothes for himself in preparation of taking Rio's place in the bathroom. Passing Rio as the boy sat down on the edge of the other bed, his slight hiss of pain halted Mick in his tracks.

"What's wrong?"

Rio grimaced and ran slim fingers lightly over his left knee. "There's something jabbing me. I get this sharp pain when I bend my knee."

"Let me see," Mick insisted. "Pull up your pant leg."

He was actually mildly surprised when Rio obeyed without a fuss. Kneeling down in front of him, he set his fingers to the pale skin of Rio's knee and gently probed the area. When one finger pressed into the flesh near his kneecap, Rio repeated his hiss of pain.

"Ow! That hurts!"

"I feel a lump," Mick told him. "When you first came into the bar your hands and knees were bleeding. I saw you pick a piece of glass out of your hand. Could be you've got some glass stuck in your knee."

Rio's face flushed scarlet and he lowered his head until his eyes were hidden by the concealing fall of his bangs. Mick could practically smell the kid's shame.

"There was a broken bottle in the parking lot. He made me crawl through the glass. Like the fucking gravel didn't hurt enough."

"Hey." Mick lightly squeezed Rio's leg. "Don't beat yourself up over something you couldn't prevent or control. He was stronger than you. You did what you had to. It's done. Let it go." Mick rubbed his thumb over the slight lump in Rio's knee. "As for this, I'm afraid the only way to get rid of it is to cut it out. Your flesh has grown over it, but if it is glass it's just going to keep cutting you from the inside every time you move. That's got to be painful as hell, especially if it's working itself deeper, which seems to be the case. If it was working itself out it would be puncturing your skin and bleeding."

Rio sighed and raised his face enough to meet Mick's eyes. His eyes were filled with a kind of mournful resignation. "I don't suppose you have some Novocain and a scalpel on you, do you?"

"No, but I've got a sharp pocket knife."

Shoulders sagging, Rio softly cursed, "That fucking figures. All right. Do it."

"Now wait a minute," Mick said, seriously backpedaling when a flare of alarm made his stomach clench. "I was kidding. If you'll wait till we get back to Indiana, there's a clinic in Indy that can take care of it for you. Or I can try to find a place around here."

"I want it out now," Rio insisted.

"What's the rush?"

"Every time it digs into me, it's him. It's him hurting me again. I want it out. I want it gone." With every word, Rio's voice rose, his tone holding an edge of panic.

"All right, all right, just calm down," Mick urged softly, hoping to soothe him. "It's not really that way, you know. What's in your knee is just an inanimate object. Sutter's gone."

"But it's because of him that it's there. Please. I'll...I'll beg if you want me to," Rio offered, though his entire body had gone stiff and he lowered his gaze to the floor.

Mick's shock was instantaneous. For one so stubborn and strong-willed it was totally out of character. Just the fact that he was willing to lower himself to do it let Mick know how important it was to him to get rid of the thing that Sutter's cruelty had caused to be stuck in his flesh. It also made Mick angry that he'd obviously felt the need to offer. Had he been beaten down so low or was Rio honestly comparing him to Sutter? Did he really come across as the type of person who would demand someone beg for his help?

His irritation made Mick's reply harsher than it had to be. "Fuck that. Like I'd ask you to beg me. I'm not the asshole Sutter was, and you need to try cultivating some pride."

Rio's head came up sharply, his cheeks flaming with humiliation. "You try having pride when you have nothing! It's a luxury you can't afford and one few people will grant you."

Unpleasantly reminded once again of Tuttle's warning about the need for diplomacy, Mick silently cursed himself. It struck him that this kid's knowledge of the world was far greater than his years could account for, and it made Mick wonder just what the boy had been through to cultivate such wisdom at his age. Most likely it had been nothing good.

Contrite, Mick expressed his regret. "My last remark was uncalled for," he admitted gruffly. "I apologize."

With suspicion in his eyes, Rio steadily met Mick's gaze then abruptly nodded.

Reaching into his pocket, Mick brought out the pocket knife he carried. It had two blades, one sharp and one blunt. He mostly carried it because the blunt one came in handy for use as a screwdriver. He opened the sharp blade and considered the razor-like edge with a fair amount of reluctance. "I'll go wash this. Be right back."

In the bathroom he caught his own gaze in the mirror. This was definitely something he didn't want to do, and his thoughts were clearly reflected in his eyes. Considering a werewolf's resistance to infection, washing the blade of his pocket knife was obviously a delaying tactic. He was glad the kid probably didn't realize it. It was one thing to inflict damage with teeth and claws during a fight, but this? To deliberately cut into someone? For this task he felt woefully unprepared, especially where it concerned the kid who waited for him in the next room.

It was his concern for Rio's emotional state that was the biggest part of the problem. The kid was feisty, mouthy and had backbone as well as a lot of heart. Those things were evident in the way he was able to keep functioning in the face of all he'd been through. Yet for all of his bravado, there was a bruised and haunted look in Rio's eyes that had imprinted itself on Mick's psyche. It had him wanting to do something to ease that hurt, but repairing damage to the human spirit wasn't something he had a lot of practice with. Lord knew he had issues of his own he preferred to bury rather than deal with. So instead of being able to offer comfort he was being asked to inflict even more physical damage on Rio. Even if it would ultimately help, it was the last thing he wanted to do.

Torn by conflicting desires, but resigned to at least doing this much for the boy, he gathered a few things, finished up at the sink, and returned to find Rio exactly as he'd left him. Mick knelt on the floor in front of him. Capturing Rio's gaze, he asked with every ounce of earnest concern he could muster, "Are you absolutely sure about this?"

"Yes."

"It's going to fucking hurt like hell. You know that, don't you?"

"I know, but it will heal fast, right?"

"Yes, but you're going to have to hold still no matter what. I can't do this and fight you at the same time."

"All right."

"Damn. I was really hoping you'd back down," Mick confessed. "Lift your leg up a little." Rio complied and Mick slid the folded towel he'd brought with him beneath Rio's knee and draped the edges loosely around the front of his leg.

"What's that for?" Rio asked.

"The blood," Mick frankly answered. He wasn't above making the coming ordeal sound as bad as possible if it would make Rio change his mind. All he got was a small

"Oh" in reply. He handed Rio the damp washcloth he'd rolled into a tube.

"What do I do with this?"

"Bite down on it. I don't think you screaming is going to go over very well with the neighbors, and honestly maybe it'll keep you from biting your own tongue."

"Jeez. You sure the hell aren't going to sugarcoat it for me, are you?"

"Why would I? This is going to fucking suck for both of us."

Rio's gaze solidly met Mick's and he could almost feel the weight of the young man's silent searching. His eyes widened slightly, realization dawning in those clear silver-gray depths, and Mick wondered just what it was the kid discovered in his eyes. Without taking his gaze from Mick's, Rio reached out, took the washcloth, opened his mouth and bit down on it.

Shaking his head and inwardly cursing, Mick curled his hand around Rio's shin just below his knee and pressed his leg firmly against the bed. Rio jumped, and Mick felt the reflexive move of muscles under his hand. It was more than apparent that Rio's first instinct was to pull away, but he quickly settled.

"You ready?" Mick asked.

Rio took a deep breath of air in through his nose, fisted his hands against the edge of the mattress and nodded.

Not wanting to draw it out, Mick applied the burnished steel of his knife to Rio's unmarked flesh and made a quick cut that was long and deep. The knife blade grated against the hard object lodged in Rio's knee, and he jerked and uttered a muffled scream. His entire body went rigid, but he made no effort to get away. Blood immediately welled up and out of the wound, flowing down to soak into the towel. Probing into the open gash, Mick found the offending object. Closing his finger and thumb around it, he found out for himself that it was indeed glass when the sharp edges cut into his skin. His blood mingled with Rio's.

"Fuck," he hissed. His first reaction was to let go, but he held on to the glass, pulling it free even as it bit deeper into his own flesh.

His fingers cleared Rio's wound with a sucking slurp and he dropped the rough shard of glass into a fold of the towel. Taking up a free edge of fabric, he pressed the towel against Rio's knee, holding it in place with his cut finger and thumb while putting pressure on the incision he'd made as well as on his own small wounds. Allowing a few moments to pass, he pulled the towel away. The flow of blood had slowed. Beneath the red-stained terry fabric, Rio's flesh had begun to knit itself together. In a matter of moments all that would remain would be a faint line to show where Mick had sliced into that pale, perfect skin. A glance at his wounded finger and thumb showed the same. He started slightly when Rio's hand grabbed his.

Breathing rapidly through his nostrils as though he'd just run a race, the boy stared at Mick's hand, watching the flesh repair itself, his gray eyes showing the shock of passing pain. Spitting the washcloth from his mouth, he licked dry lips then managed to husk out, "It cut you."

"Yeah, it did," Mick admitted with a forced smile. Feeling a little shaky from performing makeshift surgery and hating this unexpected weakness, he sat back on his heels. "It's okay. It's healing already."

Wide gray eyes stared into his. "I'm sorry. I know you didn't want to do this. Are you...all right?"

"I'm fine," Mick replied, surprised at Rio's concern. "Now I know why I never wanted to be a doctor." The tentative smile that curved Rio's lips transformed his face, and his fresh, sweet beauty took Mick's breath away.

He let go of Mick's hand. "You look a little pale. You're not gonna pass out, are you?"

The question made Mick sniff with disdain even as he reined in the involuntary wave of arousal that small smile caused. He was silently grateful for the fact that as an unshifted were, Rio's senses, while sharpening, weren't as acute as they soon would be. He couldn't yet detect the fact that he was stirring Mick's libido. "Hardly. If anyone passed out, I figured it would be you."

"As if," Rio scoffed. "Compared to some of the stuff I've been through lately" -- his smile faded and his voice lost its cocky air -- "that was nothing."

Not knowing what to say, Mick awkwardly patted his leg and rose. "Let's clean up this mess."

In the bathroom, blood was washed away and the blood-soiled towel, along with Rio's old, torn and dirty clothes, were wrapped in the plastic liner from the trash can under the sink. "I'll find another place to dispose of these," Mick explained. "I don't want the maid to find this stuff after we leave. God knows what conclusion she'd come to."

"Probably not a good one," Rio answered and yawned. He put down the towel he'd been using to dry his knee and let the overly baggy leg of the sweatpants he was wearing fall back into place.

"Why don't you hit the sack? I'm going to take a quick shower and do the same," Mick told him.

Following Mick and suppressing another yawn, Rio nodded. "Okay."

Grabbing the pair of sweats and the T-shirt he'd left on the bed, Mick went back into the bathroom and closed the door behind him. After quickly stripping, he stepped into the tub. He turned the water on, adjusted the temperature then flipped the toggle to start the shower. A groan rumbled up from the depths of his chest as the almost too hot water pelted over his scalp and ran down his body. Tension seeped out of his muscles with the heat that penetrated them. Bending his head forward, he let the water pound against the back of his neck.

"Damn, that feels good," he muttered.

After particularly tough assignments, especially those that involved life-threatening situations, a hot shower usually became the prelude to orgasm. The way the water played over his nerve endings resembled warm, wet caresses and true to form, his cock thickened and rose. Automatically he took himself in hand and with a few strokes brought his cock to full, throbbing hardness.

Mick twisted around to face the wall, letting the water continue to flow over the nape of his neck and back. The warm cascade embraced and sheltered him. Reaching for the motel soap, he lathered his hand, replaced the soap and took hold of his eager erection. With his other hand braced against the shower wall, he leaned forward a bit with his back slightly bowed. Eyes closed, he breathed in the steamy air. The bathroom became a concealing cave, the shower a soothing waterfall. His slippery hand traveled up and down the hard bar of his cock, spurring on his need to come. Breathing harder, Mick gave himself over to the sensations that were building in his groin. His conscious mind floated free, his thoughts wandering where they would until a face appeared in the darkness behind his closed lids.

She wasn't an unforgettable beauty, the woman who had been his wife. Pretty, yes, but in an average sort of way. Madelyn's strengths were centered more in her disposition. She'd loved life and made those around her love it too, at least during the time they were in her company. Her face remained so clear in Mick's memory. He could still see her smile, hear her laughter. The way it made her blue eyes sparkle had always brought a smile to his own lips. He remembered the way she'd tilt her head in just that certain way when she'd tease him and the way her chestnut-colored hair would slide through his fingers like raw silk, shimmering where the light touched it. The memory of that gleam seemed to gather and grow until the brightness flared inside his head with enough strength to make him wince.

Mick paused the movement of his hand, the ache in his chest making it hard to breathe. His erection began to flag until that memory-induced flare of light receded to a soft glow that played over lengths of platinum hair. Another face formed in his mind's eye. Rio. That troubled, newly made pup with the face of an angel. Mick's body tensed in denial and he wavered between wanting and guilt. Wanting won out. He took a deep breath and slowly released it. The next breath brought with it a reawakening to the steamy haze of warmth provided by the shower of water he stood beneath and as quickly as it had come, the tension flowed out of him.

He thought back to earlier in the evening, of that moment when he'd held Rio on his lap. He remembered the satiny strands of Rio's hair against his cheek and the unique scent of him. What would it be like to kiss those tempting lips and to caress that pale ivory skin? Mick imagined how the pillowy softness of Rio's lips against his own would feel before they'd part to allow his tongue inside the moist cavern of his mouth. He could only dream of what delectable flavors he would find within the soft warmth behind Rio's luscious lips. Would he be shy and passive, or would he boldly wrap his arms around Mick's neck and return his kisses in equal measure? Bold, he would most definitely be bold. There was strength in that slim body as well as in the spirit it contained. Not only would he accept Mick's kisses, he'd fight for an equal share in them.

Would he gasp and whimper at every touch to his body? Would his moans be husky and alluring? Yes. In this fantasy Mick created, yes. Rio would arch into his touch and beg for more. Soft, warm flesh would shift beneath Mick's fingertips with the flexing of Rio's muscles as he sought more contact. He would cry out his pleasure when Mick enclosed Rio's rigid cock within the milking confines of his fist, and he would explode with the most pleasurably devastating climax he'd ever experienced when Mick took Rio's solid length into his mouth, sucking him free of seed, of strength, of need.

Mick groaned as his arousal returned with a vengeance. Breathing hard, he gave his cock the vigorous strokes it craved. With his desires fully reawakened, he replaced thoughts of Rio with vague images of acts performed between nameless, faceless bodies. He refused to involve Rio further in his masturbation fantasies. The things that ran though his mind were enough to keep his passion aflame, and he immersed himself in the physical sensations. Pressure and heat and need gathered in his belly and below. The familiar tingle and ache built at the base of his spine and in his balls as they drew up tight. The sensations grew sharp and powerful and suddenly burst free. Intense pleasure made his body seize, wringing rich spurts of pearly seed from his cock. The muscles in his abdomen rippled while creamy stripes and dots were laid against the shower wall, the final weaker spurts dribbling over Mick's fingers.

With forehead laid against the shower wall a name fell like a whispered wish from his lips. "Rio." The hand that lay braced against the shower wall curled into a fist. "No," Mick denied, admonishing himself for his weakness. The pain of losing Maddy was enough to last a lifetime. He wouldn't accept another lover. Especially not some traumatized kid who needed protection, not fornication.

He opened his eyes but kept his thoughts at bay by concentrating on the sound of his own panting breaths. When they returned to normal, he quickly finished his shower, toweled off, and donned the sweatpants, opting to forgo wearing the T-shirt as well. A few extra swipes with an unused hand towel saw his hair mostly dried, and, draping the towel over the tub, he flipped a switch, killing the bathroom light before opening the door. Rio had turned all the lights off except a floor lamp that stood by the table across the room. Crossing to it, Mick turned the small knob beneath the bulb and plunged the room into darkness.

Pale ribbons of light from the tall overhead fixtures on the poles that bordered the parking lot filtered in from around the edges of the drapes, but for someone with night vision as acute as his, it was hardly necessary. He walked to the bed that would be his for the night and traversed the small aisle between it and the second bed. Curled on his side, Rio was sound asleep. Mick closed his eyes and listened to the boy's slow, measured breaths. He scented the air and caught the warm, clean essence of Rio's distinctive musk.

A wave of guilt and longing swept over him that brought not only remorse but a perverse sense of defiance as well. Before his brain could even begin to analyze what he was feeling, a jaw-cracking yawn caught him, and shaking his head, he determinedly drew down the covers on his bed. Now was not the time for self-analysis. He rolled into bed, bunched the pillow under his cheek and settled comfortably on his left side with his back to Rio. Exhaustion pulled at him and in a matter of seconds he embraced sleep.

He woke several hours later to harsh mumbling cries and the restless stirring of a body moving beneath the blankets that covered it. Rio was dreaming. Instantly awake, Mick sat up and watched him for a moment, debating a course of action. He didn't want to wake the kid if the dream turned out to be something that would subside on its own. The debate was over when Rio screamed.

Mick was out of his own bed before his head realized his body was moving. He reached for Rio and laid a hand on his shoulder to give him a shake. "Wake up, kid. It's just a dream," he rumbled in a sleep-roughened voice.

"No!" Rio yelled as he tried to roll away.

Mick halted his move, pulled Rio up into a sitting position and brought him tight against his chest. "Rio, stop. Breathe. Breathe in." He shoved his wrist under Rio's nose. "Smell," he growled.

Whether it was his firm order that got through or his scent, Mick didn't know, but after taking a deep breath, Rio sagged against him. "It's you," he mumbled and wound his slim arms around Mick's torso.

"Yeah, it's me. You awake now?" Mick softly muttered. He tried to get a look at Rio's face, but the kid had bent his head and nestled his cheek against Mick's bare chest.

Mick shook his head and sighed. His idea had worked all too well. Even in sleep, a startled wolf would automatically use his nose to identify the threat. Mick figured if Rio caught his scent, he'd at least feel at ease enough to let his nightmare go. Trouble was, he'd been too successful. Rio was clinging to him like a limpet and giving no signs of letting go. When he tried to loosen the kid's grasp, Rio merely uttered a few plaintive moans and held on even tighter.

Tired and resigned to being stuck, Mick maneuvered around until he was able to lie down. Apparently satisfied, Rio loosened his grip somewhat and, sprawling across Mick, went totally boneless. The kid was acting just like a wolf pup that, not only for warmth but for security's sake, would curl around his elders while sleeping. Mick figured once Rio had woken up he'd be yelling at him to get away, but apparently being half asleep had lowered the kid's human instincts in favor of those of the wolf. The wolf with his intensely primitive sense of self-preservation felt safe with him; therefore, so did the human.

There was only one other explanation for Rio's acceptance of him, and Mick wasn't about to entertain that notion. He had yawned, closed his eyes and started to fall asleep when a wordless idea whispered through his mind. *Mate.* The smug satisfaction radiating from that part of him that was wolf pissed him off, but he was too exhausted and too comfortable to try denying it. Perversely, he wrapped his arms around Rio and had just enough time to register how right it felt to lie here with him before he fell asleep.

* * *

Rio blinked a few times, then woke with a start. His entire body had gone rigid until the sights before his wide eyes registered in his brain. Slowly, ever so slowly, taut muscles eased and his harsh breaths slowed. Motel room. He was in a motel room with that guy, Mick, who'd freed him from a nightmare become real. The bastard who'd held him prisoner for the past few torturous weeks was dead.

That thought now left him strangely unmoved. The night before, when Sutter had been killed, Rio's emotions had twirled around in dizzying spirals that made his head spin. He'd been elated to be free and furious because of what had been done to him. Remembering how he had kicked the man's dead body over and over again brought with it a sense of shock. He'd just been so damned angry. He'd had to express it or go mad. Rio normally wasn't the vindictive or violent type; it wasn't in his nature to wish ill upon others, but the extreme pain Sutter had put him through had made him wish the man who'd turned and tormented him was dead. Now that it was done, he took no great satisfaction from it. The reality left him feeling merely numb and lost.

*What am I going to do?*

That question was one he'd never seriously considered while being used as Sutter's "toy." He'd almost given up hope of being able to run from the sick bastard. Planning for the future had seemed like an exercise in futility. Sutter had kept Rio at his side most of the time and caged whenever he left Rio on his own. Most of Rio's mental processes had been engaged in merely working to please Sutter so as not to be punished. Whenever he was left alone he was too exhausted to think about devising a plan to get away. Escape had seemed impossible and help wasn't forthcoming from any of those people Sutter had called his pack. They'd all turned a blind eye to what was happening to him. He wanted to hate them for that, but the new, instinctive knowledge waking inside made him understand why they'd let Sutter have his way. He was alpha, and that meant he was godlike in the hierarchy of the wolf.

A chill shot down his spine when he remembered the dead boy Mick had mentioned after his fight with Sutter. That crazy wacko had actually killed someone. Someone he'd tormented in the same way as Rio. To think that he would have suffered the same fate, if the CFSBE enforcer hadn't stepped in, made Rio feel sick. He'd willfully avoided accepting the possibility that Sutter would ultimately cause his death. Realizing now that Sutter would have killed him was so chilling he was actually glad he'd managed to convince himself that it wouldn't happen. Now that he knew for sure that it was only a matter of time before Sutter disposed of him in some horrific manner, he could only imagine how much worse things would have gotten.

These thoughts stirred his emotions and when hot tears leaked from his eyes, he made no effort to stop them. He wanted to go home so badly. He wanted things to be the way they were when his mother was alive. They'd been a family. They'd been happy. Rio knew his dad had probably worried himself sick when he disappeared and the pain of that thought stabbed deep. Still, however much his leaving had hurt, staying would have hurt his father even more.

And now here he was with nothing and nowhere to go. It didn't take a genius to figure that his room at the boarding house had probably already been cleaned out. Not being there to pay the weekly rent would have led the landlord to believe he'd moved out. So what if his meager possessions had been left behind? The man knew what he did to make money. If something happened to one of his boarders while turning tricks, he'd probably consider it none of his business.

The reality of knowing that he was back to having absolutely nothing was depressing in the extreme. Accompanied by the realization that he'd been turned into a werewolf, it made his stomach clench. Chill terror threatened to overwhelm him. Rio forced himself to breathe evenly and let go of the tension that made his muscles go tight. Those nights when his body had tried to change had been horrific. The excruciating pain had been second only to the horror of feeling his bones and flesh shifting and squirming like some alien creature was trying to burst free of his body. Only the knowledge now that there was someone who'd help him when the change came saved him from going off the deep end. That Mick guy had said so, hadn't he?

Taking a stuttering breath, Rio caught a whiff of a scent that lingered on the pillow beneath his cheek. Sharp images and impressions flooded his mind, and he suddenly remembered the events that took place after he went to bed. The nightmare. It had invaded his sleeping mind and began with him being back in that cursed cage with Sutter coming for him. The man's hulking figure had appeared in the doorway of the cellar room where he'd been held, but Sutter came no closer. Rio waited in an agony of suspense until, without warning, shards of glass had come flying at him from every direction. Fear welled inside him and all he could hear was the sound of Sutter's laughter.

In his dream he'd fought to get away, throwing himself against the bars of the cage while random slices appeared on his skin and bright blood had flowed until all he could see was red. He remembered screaming, the sound pulling him out of his nightmare. Strong arms had appeared out of nowhere and were suddenly holding him against a warm, solid body. There'd been a voice that soothed and a scent that made all the pain and terror disappear and, instead of being alone, he was being held and comforted. A feeling of unquestioning trust had bubbled up inside, and all the bad things had melted away as he drifted back to sleep.

Rio took a deep breath. It was this scent that had calmed his fears, the one that permeated this fabric. He rubbed his cheek against the pillow until it suddenly dawned on him just what he was doing. A frown formed between his brows.

Since when did he trust anyone? Feeling like a wimp and silently scoffing at the notion before he could even consider it, he threw the covers back, wiped his eyes and sat up. It was then he realized that he was alone in the room. A glance at the clock radio on the nightstand showed the time to be after 10:00 a.m. Feeling a small spurt of panic when it occurred to him that he might have been abandoned, he jumped out of bed.

The other bed had been slept in, but there was nothing else to show that anyone had shared this room with him. There were no scattered possessions or clothing anywhere. Intent on seeing if the vehicle that had carried him here was still in the parking lot, he started to cross the carpeted expanse that stood between him and the closed drapes at the front windows. Before he reached them, he spotted Mick's duffel and laptop case lying on the floor on the far side of the second bed and profound relief settled over him. Wherever he'd gone, Mick would be back. He wouldn't leave without taking his stuff with him.

With that steadying thought in mind, Rio retreated to the bathroom and after taking care of business, he washed up and settled in to wait. Back on the bed with the remote in hand and much like Mick had done the night before, he began flipping through the channels.

Half an hour later he heard the sound of a vehicle coming to a stop in the parking lot outside the room, and a few minutes after that a door on the vehicle was slammed shut. For some reason he couldn't force himself to go see if it was his rescuer. Gaze on the television, he waited almost breathlessly, his ears straining for every sound. A sigh of relief passed his lips and the tension in his shoulders eased when he heard a muffled curse along with some fumbling touches to the outer door handle. Apparently Mick was having trouble getting in.

A smile tried to form on his lips from the happy zing of feeling that shot through him, but Rio forced a frown instead and bounced off the bed. A few barefoot steps brought him to the door and he opened it. His eyes met Mick's and his heart stuttered when a pleased smile met his appearance. With everything so fucked up the night before he hadn't really noticed much about the guy who'd rescued him. *Damn, he was tall.* Rio had to lift his chin to meet those piercing blue-green eyes. Mick's dark hair was being teased by a slight breeze, and under the sunlight, those shifting strands revealed deep auburn and mahogany highlights. For a moment, Rio was mesmerized by their shimmer until Mick's words stirred him into action.

"Good, you're up. Help me with this stuff, would you?" Mick asked. He was juggling a cardboard carrier with drinks, a couple of fast food bags, and several other plastic bags with various store logos on them.

Rio took the drink carrier, righting the cups that were threatening to spill over, as well as the food bags. He carried them to the table and heard Mick enter and shut the door behind him. Moving around to the far side of the table, he watched his rescuer walk toward him. That short distance was crossed with a few confident strides and Rio actually felt somewhat disoriented seeing the trim, broad-shouldered man approaching him.

If not for the scent, he wouldn't have been sure this was the same man. His awareness of Mick the night before had been limited by his own emotional issues. This morning the blinders were off and...wow. Rio was shocked to realize the guy was just plain hot. For the first time in what seemed like a long, long while, his libido sat up and took notice, which was all well and good until he remembered what happened after he went to sleep. Knowing they'd shared a bed and that this guy, practically a stranger, had held him like some scaredy-cat, blubbering baby who'd made such a fuss about having a nightmare, was just plain embarrassing. Fortunately Mick didn't seem to be paying attention to the flush that heated Rio's cheeks. He was busy removing items from the bags of food.

"I did some shopping and stopped for breakfast. Let's eat before it gets cold," Mick said.

The mention of food suddenly made Rio aware of just how hungry he was, and his embarrassment was swept aside in favor of eating. Like the night before, they sat at the table, divided up the food and dug in. Mick had brought pancakes and bacon with hash brown patties along with breakfast English-style muffins filled with eggs, cheese, and sausage. Just like last night's meal, it all tasted so good Rio couldn't resist stuffing himself. A soft drink and a cup of coffee were pushed in his direction along with the food.

"I didn't know if you drank coffee or not so I got you both," Mick told him after swallowing a mouthful of food.

Rio nodded. "Yeah, I drink coffee. Is there any cream?"

"Check the bags," Mick directed him. "I threw cream and sugar in one of them."

Ignoring the sugar, Rio found the cream and emptied several of the small, sealed containers into his coffee cup. "Thanks. And um, thanks for the food."

"You're welcome. When you finish eating you can try on the clothes I bought you. There was a little mall not too far from here, so I got you some stuff at a couple of the stores. I wasn't sure what size you needed, but one of the sales clerks was about your height and weight so we guesstimated."

Blinking in surprise, Rio looked at Mick, who simply shrugged.

"Told you I was going to get you some clothes. I didn't figure you'd want to walk barefoot into a store dressed in my stuff. There are shoes too. Your foot was hanging out from under the covers so I sort of measured it against the sole of my shoe. Whatever doesn't fit I'll exchange before we leave...get you something that fits right." Mick took a swallow of coffee. "Oh, and I got you a toothbrush and some other stuff."

Mick went back to his food and Rio lowered his gaze to the table. He was confused by the rush of emotions that assaulted him. Part of him wanted to be pissed that Mick had so high-handedly decided on what clothes and things to buy him, while another part was amazed at his generosity. Since he'd left home no one had given him anything unless there was some kind of condition attached, and it was that thought that made suspicion raise its ugly head. Rio tilted his chin, sending a cynical sideways glance toward Mick.

At that moment Mick happened to look over and their eyes met. Mick frowned. "What?"

After of moment of saying nothing, Rio finally replied. "What do you want?"

"Want? What do you mean?"

"What do I have to do in return for the clothes?"

Understanding dawned in Mick's eyes and his expression went from relaxed and friendly to cold and stiff. "Not a damn thing but accept them." Mouth opening to say something more, he stopped, closed his eyes for a moment and took a deep breath. Rio could see the man visibly reining himself in. When he opened his eyes he continued in a voice that had completely lost its earlier warmth. "I'm not trying to buy you, kid. Is that how you've been getting by the last couple of years? You been selling yourself?"

Rio stiffened with shamed outrage. He wasn't happy with the things he'd done to pay his way in the world, but to have someone so baldly ask that question was like a knife to the gut. He stood up so quickly his chair flipped back and fell with a muffled thud against the carpet. Looking Mick straight in the eye, he yelled, "None of your goddamned fucking business!" and with no other place to go, he marched into the bathroom and slammed the door shut.

Putting his back against that barrier, Rio slid to the floor until he was sitting on the cold tiles. Dry-eyed, he stared bleakly at nothing while helpless anger surged through him. He hated this shit. When was all this fucking crap going to stop? It was all her fault. His stepmother. *God, how he hated her.*

It wasn't like he'd had a lot of options when he'd left home. He'd tried to find a real job but he'd been too young. When that first guy had offered him money to suck his dick,

Rio had been tired, homeless, and hungry. The money had been a temptation he couldn't refuse. Was that so bad? It wasn't like he liked it or anything, but he had to have a place to stay and food to eat. All that cost money. His only other choice was to go home and that he could never do. Things had gotten to the point where he couldn't even look his dad in the eye.

Rio sat there silently stewing until Mick's voice came from beyond the door, making him jump. The warmth in that voice that had fled at Rio's unfair assumption had returned. "Hey, kid. I wasn't trying to pass judgment on you or make you feel bad. I know you did what you had to do to survive. Jeez, I've got no room to throw stones. Look at me, I killed a man yesterday. Just because it can be argued that what I did was legal because of my job doesn't make it right. Even a lowlife son of a bitch like him had a right to a fair trial, but I took that away. I've done other things too. Believe me, I'm no sweet-smelling, unsullied rose. Everybody's got something in their life they think they have to hide. Things they're not proud of having done. That's just the way it is."

As quickly as his anger had ignited, it now burned away. At a slow, grudging pace Rio got to his feet and eased open the door. Just on the other side, Mick stood waiting. Rio silently eyed him for a moment then asked, "What else have you done? Something you're not proud of." He really didn't know why he wanted to know except that maybe knowing that Mick had things like that in his life too would make it easier somehow for Rio to deal with his own shit.

"I threw a baseball through old Mrs. Washburn's window. On purpose," Mick confessed with a wry smile.

That unexpected answer caused an answering smile to tug at Rio's lips. "Why?"

"'Cause she was a mean old bitch who set out poison for the neighborhood cats. She didn't like them shitting in her flower beds."

"You should have just beaned her with that ball." Mick's snort of laughter made Rio grin.

"My dad really *would* have done more than just blister my ass."

"Is that what happened?"

"Yeah."

"That's not fair."

"Yeah, well, you know dads. They have to at least pretend to do what's right as an example to their kids. Truth is, he didn't like the old biddy either."

Rio nodded. "Yeah. My dad, he…" Stung by what he'd nearly blurted out, Rio stopped before finishing. Sharing his problems with someone was something he'd never done and it puzzled him that he wanted to do it now. Why? Why to this guy, who was little better than a stranger?

"Hey, look," Mick said softly, drawing Rio's attention. "If there's anything you want to talk about, it goes no further than me. I'm no psychologist or anything, but sometimes it helps to talk about things, just to get it off your chest. You know?"

Rio nodded but said nothing. Things were edging into dangerous ground again. To talk meant to trust, and he so wasn't ready for that.

"Anyway," Mick went on, "How about you try these clothes on and get ready to go. If we leave here in the next hour or so we can be at my place by ten tonight."

"All right."

Rio accepted the bags Mick handed him and retreated back into the bathroom. Even guessing at sizes, Mick had done well. There were two pairs of soft stonewashed jeans and two T-shirts, one dark blue and the other deep cherry red. Along with the toiletries there were socks and underwear. Rio gratefully used the toothbrush then got dressed. After brushing his hair, he donned socks and new athletic shoes. Everything fit just right, and he couldn't suppress the bashful smile that curved his lips when he stepped out of the bathroom.

"Hey, stuff fits. Good guessing, huh?" Mick observed, while giving Rio the once-over.

"Yeah. Thanks."

"No problem. Well, now I know if ever get tired of being an enforcer for the CFSBE I could always become a personal shopper."

Rio raised one brow in disbelief.

"I agree," Mick concurred, correctly interpreting that look. "I don't believe it either. You ready to go? Did you use the potty? I don't want to have to stop fifteen minutes into the trip 'cause you gotta pee."

"Shut up, and yeah, I'm ready to go."

Mick chuckled. "I'm going to the head a minute. You take this and pack your other stuff in it." He handed Rio a duffel bag similar to the one he had his own clothes in.

Having things to pack gave Rio a sense of security, a sense of simply being. Even the most meager of possessions served as an anchor. To have nothing had left him feeling adrift and questioning his very existence. It was such a small thing and in reality probably didn't rate the importance he placed on it, but everyone had something that gave them their own perception of being real. He supposed his quirky reasoning was no sillier than that of anyone else.

Mick emerged from the bathroom, and the two of them took up their respective bags, stowed them in the back of Mick's SUV and hit the road. The drive was uneventful. Long stretches of time on the highway were interrupted by a couple of breaks at rest stops. Lunch was more fast food, but dinner was eaten at a popular steak house, one of a well-known, nationwide chain. Mick claimed he wanted a "real" meal and Rio had no problem going along with him. His order of barbecue ribs, baked potato with butter and sour cream, accompanied by Caesar salad and dinner rolls, went down with considerable ease.

It's too bad the waitress had to put a damper on his improving mood by flirting with Mick. She'd even had the temerity to tell Mick that his little brother was cute. Cute! What the fuck? Was he a puppy or something? Still, her flirting had made Rio take greater notice of Mick. He couldn't help but see that the waitress wasn't the only one shooting admiring glances his way. That some of those glances were meant for Rio himself, he ignored. He'd seen too many looks like those. They'd led to deals made in back alleys that ate away at his self-esteem one bite at a time. At least while he was in the enforcer's company he wouldn't have to worry about such things.

During the entire length of the long drive the silence between them was filled in by tunes on the radio. Rio discovered that he and Mick had similar tastes in music. Fortunately. Nothing made for a more unpleasant trip than having to listen to music you couldn't connect with.

There wasn't much in the way of conversation between them, mostly comments made about the passing scenery or the drivers around them. Rio dozed off and on, each time waking with a start until he got his bearings. If Mick noticed his abrupt awakenings, he didn't mention it. He didn't ask any questions of Rio either. Apparently he meant what he said about being there to listen if Rio wanted to talk, but he wasn't going to push the issue. The easy silence between them allowed Rio to relax and drop his guard. Unfortunately, it also gave him time to brood and the thoughts that plagued him weren't happy ones. They churned inside him but had no place to go.

After eight plus hours on the road, Mick received a call on his cell phone. Though the sun had just set, it was still fairly bright outside.

"Matranga," Mick answered after picking the phone up from its resting place in a console cubbyhole.

Rio glanced over at him. He appeared relaxed, but Rio could see the subtle tension that took hold as he listened to what his caller was saying. The hand holding on to the steering wheel tightened; his fingers flexed several times.

"Sure, I've known Bryce for years. We play poker a couple times a month." Mick listened for a moment. "Okay. Then he's expecting us?" Another moment of silence was followed by, "We're about an hour out. Should I call him or will you let him know?" Mick waited for a response then replied. "All right. Bye."

Mick replaced his cell phone, took a quick look in Rio's direction then turned his gaze back to the road. "That was Booth, my boss. He's found a place for you."

A thrill of apprehension made Rio's stomach clench. "What are you talking about? I thought I was going to your place."

"You were, but it would have been temporary. You need a longer-term situation."

Rebellion flared. "Why? I've been on my own for almost three years. I can take care of myself," Rio insisted, glaring at Mick.

"I agree that to a certain extent you were getting by, but things have changed. You're a werewolf now. Remember what I told you in the bar? You're untrained and unprotected. I can't just cut you loose to fend for yourself. You think the predators after young humans are bad? Now that you're a werewolf, you've got a new set of worries to deal with. There are some paranormals out there who consider pups like you delectable prey. You need the shield a pack will provide, and that's what's been set up for you. My friend, Bryce, is alpha of a pack in the Indianapolis area. He's agreed to take you in."

At the mention of the word "alpha," Rio blanched. Sutter had been an alpha and look how being under his thumb had turned out. The last thing he wanted was to deal with yet another arrogant, sadistic asshole who bore the same title. "I don't want to go there."

"Kid --" Mick began.

"Stop calling me kid," Rio ground out. "I'll be nineteen in two weeks."

"Yeah, a real grown-up," Mick answered, his voice laden with sarcasm. Pausing for a moment, he began again in a more reasonable tone. "Sorry about the grown-up comment but, regardless of what you want, this is what you need. You'll have someone to show you the ropes, make sure you know the ins and outs of what it means to be a were and how to avoid the pitfalls. Most importantly, when your first change comes you'll have someone to help you with it."

Rio remained stubbornly silent.

"Look, there's no reason to get bent out of shape. Bryce is nothing like Sutter. He's a good guy, and he and his people will take good care of you. I promise."

"You can make all the promises you want. That doesn't mean you can keep them," Rio said with a heavy dose of bitterness in his reply.

"Is that what happened at home?"

That softly voiced question was so unexpected, Rio answered without thinking. "When he remarried, my dad promised everything would be all right. I didn't want him to do it, but he was so happy I didn't say too much. Even though he seemed okay most of the time, I knew he was lonely. He missed Mom. Carol, this woman he met, made him happy so I tried to like her, I really did, but I just always felt uncomfortable with her."

"What happened?"

By this time the twilight had given way to the night. Being in the dark made it easier to talk, and Rio found the words flowing freely as he revealed those shameful things he'd never told anyone. "A couple of months after the wedding she starting saying things to me and touching me when dad wasn't around. I didn't know what to do. At first I was scared. I knew it was wrong but at the same time it was..."

"Exciting?"

"Yeah."

"It's only natural that your body would react, Rio, even if your head was telling you something wasn't right."

"Yeah, well, it reacted all right. One night when my dad was working late she came to my room. She got in bed with me and we..."

"Had sex."

Even now Rio was eaten up by guilt at the thought. "I couldn't stop it. I didn't know how. Afterwards I felt sick. All I could think about was how hurt my dad would be if he knew. I told her I wouldn't do it anymore, but she said if I didn't she'd tell him. She'd tell him it was my fault, and that I'd started everything. So I went along with it. I went along with that smirking, two-faced nasty bitch whore until I couldn't take it anymore. I couldn't stand to be around my dad. Having him be nice to me. I couldn't deal with how I was betraying him so I left. But the thing that hurts the most is that sometimes...even though I hated her...I liked it. I liked the sex. I came every fucking time she touched me."

Rio turned his face toward the passenger window. There wasn't much to be seen in the darkness, but it was the best he could do to satisfy his need to hide. He waited for Mick to call him the lowlife piece of scum he was. He tensed when he heard Mick's deep sigh.

"Damn. You have got one shitload of crap to deal with. You know I just have to say it. I thought this before, but now I can see how true it is. You've got a lot of backbone, Rio. I admire your courage. You take the blows and you keep trudging on. A lot of people in your situation would have crumbled under the strain by now."

Rio turned his head, his eyes wide with disbelief. Mick admired him? The idea was so preposterous he couldn't wrap his head around it. "You gotta be shitting me."

"No, I'm not. I've got no reason to lie to you. Like I said before, I'm no psychologist but my take on it is this: your stepmother is a sexual predator who took advantage of you. You were what, fourteen when all this started?"

"Yeah."

"Guys your age are walking hormones. There's no way you could not react to somebody touching you and making you feel good. As far as I can see, you don't have a reason to feel guilty about that. Your physical reaction was inescapable."

Even though he knew what Mick was telling him was true, Rio still found it hard to absolve himself of all blame.

"As for the rest of it," Mick continued, "you were an inexperienced, scared kid. I don't know what your relationship is like with your dad, but I'm thinking you should have gone to him right away when it started. Maybe it would have made a difference. But I can see why you ran away rather than try and deal with it. You did everything in your power to keep your dad from being hurt, and that's where you made your big mistake."

"Huh?"

"It's not the child's job to protect the parents. It's the other way around. While your stepmother was definitely a conniving bitch, I blame your dad for a big part of this. If he'd been paying attention like he should have, he would have known something was wrong."

"How can you say that? I hid everything. He couldn't have known," Rio snapped, not liking this attack on his dad.

"I saw the missing person's report your dad filed on you. I've seen your school records. When your mom died, your grades went in the crapper, but they came back up a few months later. That was the first indication that your grades suffered when you experienced emotional trauma. When all this started up with your stepmother, your grades took another dive. Did the school inform your dad about it? Did he get, like, report cards? Hell, do they do that anymore?"

In spite of the seriousness of their talk, Rio felt a ripple of amusement at Mick's puzzled question. "Yeah, they do and yes, my dad saw my grades."

"What did he say about them?"

"He was concerned. He asked me if I was having a problem in school, if I was getting along with the other kids and stuff."

"But he didn't ask if there was a problem at home?"

"No."

"What did you tell him?"

"That there wasn't a problem. That everything was okay."

"And yet your grades were shit until you ran."

"Yeah."

"And that's where *he* made *his* big mistake. He should have leaned on you. If you'd been my kid, I'd have hounded you until you cracked."

For the first time in he couldn't remember how long, Rio laughed. It felt surprisingly good. "Yeah, but you're a badass. My dad's just a regular guy. Is that how you treat your kids?"

"Fortunately I don't have any."

"Why fortunately?"

"Because my wife died."

Stunned at Mick's revelation, Rio uttered a small, "Oh. Sorry. How did she…shit, I shouldn't ask. Forget it."

"No, it's all right. She died in a fire. Madelyn was a firefighter. She and two others were killed in a warehouse fire when the floor collapsed under them."

"Jesus. That's awful. I guess I'm not the only one who has shit to deal with." And it suddenly struck Rio just how true that statement was. It also gave him hope that someday he'd get his life straightened around. Mick hadn't let personal tragedy ruin *his* life. From what Rio could see, he'd picked up the pieces and moved on. Not only that, he helped people. Sure, it was his job but a job he'd apparently chosen to do.

"It was rough going for a while but that was four years ago," Mick answered. "I'm pretty much all right with it now. Shit. This is it."

"What?"

"Our exit. I almost missed it," Mick explained, steering his vehicle into the right lane. "From here it's just twenty minutes to Bryce's."

Rio said nothing. The wall that had come down between him and the man at his side was suddenly back in place. While talking to Mick, the constant lump of anxiety and self-loathing he carried had loosened but now it was winding tight again. Rio was once more a prisoner to currents he had no control over, and they spun him around to suit their own whims. The relief he'd felt at finally telling someone about his stepmother disappeared. What difference did it make if one person he was no longer going to have a connection with had given him absolution? It had been a fleeting bit of forgiveness easily granted to someone who would be forgotten, and it made him feel hollow inside. Being invisible and overlooked was a feeling he'd come to know all too well.

The rest of the trip was accomplished in silence. They'd skirted Indy itself by way of the 465 bypass and ended up on the outskirts of some suburb. The houses were big and built on generous plots of land with stands of trees and brush that sheltered them from the neighbors. Mick pulled into the driveway of a sizable two-story white clapboard house with a screened-in wraparound porch and a two-car garage. The outside lights were on: one by the front door, two on the garage and one on a decorative iron pole in the middle of the yard. When they pulled in the driveway and parked, someone rose from a chair behind the screening, opened the door and after taking the two steps down from the porch, traversed a walkway to meet them.

Mick had gotten out of the vehicle, and the man stopped in front of him with a grin on his face. "I hear you've been out causing trouble again."

Rio couldn't see Mick's face, but he heard the amusement in his voice. "Trouble runs from me. Whatever Booth's been telling you, I deny."

"Yeah, right. That's going to be kind of hard when I can see some of the evidence right there." He inclined his head toward Rio.

Mick turned to him. "Rio, come on out and let me introduce you."

Reluctantly, Rio exited the SUV and joined them on the sidewalk.

"Bryce Mills, this is Rio Hardin."

The man called Bryce reached out his hand. Rio extended his own and accepted the handshake. A few inches shorter than Mick, Bryce was powerfully built and imposing. Though he wasn't overbearing the way Sutter had been, Rio could still sense his power. He had short-cropped brown hair and ordinary yet even features that were nicely put together. His smile reflected the welcome in his brown eyes and he seemed normal enough, but Rio still didn't like the idea of being near another alpha.

"Hello Rio, it's nice to meet you. We've got a room all ready for you, or maybe I should say my wife, Becky, got the room ready for you. I know you're probably a little disoriented by all this, but I hope you'll eventually be able to feel at home here."

"Thanks," Rio answered around the lump in his throat.

At the mention of Bryce's wife a thrill of alarm shot down his spine. After his experiences at Carol's hands, wives weren't on his list of favorite things either.

"Well, it's late. I should let you go get settled in," Mick said, addressing Rio. "Come on, let's get your stuff."

Rio followed Mick and after he opened the back of his vehicle, Rio grabbed his bag.

"Try to relax, okay? There's nothing to be afraid of here. You really are in good hands. Bryce and Becky will treat you well."

Rio shrugged but didn't answer Mick's earnest comments. At this point it didn't matter what anyone said. A bleak sense of depression was enveloping him. When they rejoined Bryce on the sidewalk, Rio could feel his chest tightening up. It was a struggle to continue breathing normally. Mick was leaving him here, but he couldn't put his finger on why it was such a big deal. Yeah Bryce was an alpha and had one of those dreaded things called a wife, but maybe it would be all right. It wasn't as though he wasn't used to being around strangers.

It just seemed *wrong* to be left behind, but he didn't know why. It felt as though the first dependable thing he'd had in his life in a long time was being torn away, which really didn't make sense. After all, they'd known each other less than forty-eight hours. It's not like he thought Mick was anything special. Mick's voice pulled Rio out of his private thoughts and drew Rio's gaze to him.

"Bryce, thanks a lot. I'll see you at the next poker game. At Jed's this time, right?"

"Yeah, it is and it's your turn to bring the pizza. Meat lovers, none of that chicken, pineapple crap Steve tried to foist on us last time."

"Yeah, yeah, I hear you." Mick climbed into his SUV, started it up, and rolled down the window. He looked straight at Rio. "See you, kid. You too, Bryce."

"Take it easy, Mick," Bryce answered.

Rio said nothing. He watched in silence as Mick backed his vehicle to the street and drove away. Glancing at the man who now held his fate in his hands, Rio quickly lowered his gaze and swallowed the fear that began to churn in his gut. Another alpha. He'd been left with another alpha.

"Rio?" Bryce questioned, drawing his attention. "Ready to go in?"

Wordlessly nodding, Rio sent one more longing glance in the direction of Mick's disappearing truck before turning to follow Bryce.

# Chapter Three

Mick switched the radio off and made the short trip home in absolute silence. Unease stirred in the pit of his stomach, making him feel almost nauseous. In his mind he kept seeing that bleak look on Rio's face. Had those silver-gray eyes looked close to shedding tears?

"Fuck. Get a grip, Matranga. He'll be fine," Mick muttered then shut his mouth in disgust at his own perceived overreaction.

Still, guilt pulled at him and made him angry. By the time he got home, he was good and pissed. After parking the SUV in the garage, he attempted to alleviate his mood with a few drinks, but even fifty-year-old mellow aged scotch failed to sweeten his surly disposition. Sitting in the living room with the lights out, his eyes registered the flickering lights of the television as the scenes of whatever show was on changed, but in his mind he was seeing nothing more than Rio.

He kept thinking about the things Rio had told him about his situation at home and why he'd left. Mick would bet anything the kid's dad would be overjoyed to hear from him, even if he had to face up to some nasty truths about his second wife. Knowing it was something he couldn't get involved in without Rio's permission, Mick went on to assure himself that the kid would be fine. Everything he'd told Rio about Bryce was true, and Becky really was a nice person too. She wasn't the fussy type, which was good, and she'd see to it that Rio got the care he needed with some home-cooked meals in the bargain. The kid really needed to put a few pounds on that too-slim frame.

Thinking about that, he remembered how he'd wanted to tell Bryce about getting Rio some kind of counseling. He started to reach for the phone but slapped himself down. Hell, it was after one. He could just imagine how pleased Bryce would be to hear from him at this time of night.

*When did I become a freaking mother hen?*

Shaking his head at what was surely just his brain going soft, Mick decided to go to bed. In the morning he'd go to work, file his report, make some recommendations on Rio's care based on what he'd learned from the boy and that would be that. End of story and on to the next assignment. If that pat solution left him feeling strangely bereft, he refused to acknowledge it.

\* \* \*

Over the next few days Mick was given a series of low-profile, cakewalk assignments. Booth's prediction that there would be an inquiry into Sutter's death proved accurate. Rather than send him on any missions that could take a deadly turn, Mick got to roust a pixie selling rare orchid pollen whose fellow customers, after having imbibed, had gone bananas in the butterfly enclosure of the city zoo. The naked pixie/butterfly orgy had made headlines in the local papers. After that, he'd served a warning citation on a troll who was attempting to extract a toll from people crossing a bridge in a public park. It wouldn't have been that big a deal except for the fact that this particular troll had a shoe fetish. People were a little disgruntled at having to give up their footwear. He also got to arrest an alchemist dealing in illegal penile enhancement spells.

"Jesus Christ, just go buy some fucking Viagra," he told a potential customer when he'd arrived to apprehend the offender. "At least the pills won't make your dick shrink when the effect wears off."

White-faced, the horrified man had rushed off without looking back. The alchemist had merely laughed. "Idiot humans. They still don't get the give and take of alchemy. To get, you have to give something of equal value."

"If you tried explaining it to them, maybe they'd understand."

The alchemist gestured toward the sign hanging on the wall behind the counter of his shop that clearly explained the rules. "Is it my fault they don't read?"

"Yeah, yeah. Tell it to the judge," Mick growled before hauling the guy in. After dropping the alchemist off to be booked, Mick paid a visit to his boss.

Booth was eating lunch at his desk while perusing a stack of paperwork. Mick's boss looked to be in his midthirties but in fact was closer to eighty. He was a slim man of medium height whose perpetually boyish looks went a long way toward making people underestimate him. He was also a werewolf, hence his leniency and understanding when it came to Mick's apprehension incident record. He knew from personal experience that under certain circumstances werewolves were not the most patient of people. The fact that he deliberately assigned Mick the cases most likely to erupt into violence went a long way to smoothing things over when his methods were questioned. Most paranormal species had a tendency to act on a visceral level rather than cooperate when confronted with inappropriate behavior, something Booth took great pleasure in reminding his own superiors of whenever questions arose about how things were handled.

Knowing Booth wasn't one to stand on ceremony, Mick barged into his office and flung himself down into one of the chairs in front of Booth's desk. His boss looked up, used a napkin to dab at the corners of his mouth and drawled, "If you're here to complain you can save it. The paperwork's being processed as we speak. You'll be back on regular duty in a couple of days."

"Bless the moon for that," Mick replied. "I'm about to go crazy here. You got anything good coming up? How about another one of those demon extermination cases? I liked using that flamethrower."

Booth laughed. "Sounds like you're itching for a fight. Maybe you should spend some time in the gym. I'm sure Narev would love to put you through a workout."

At the mention of the golem, Narev, Mick grinned. "I'm itching for a fight, not a beating."

"At least you're honest enough to admit you can't take him."

"I'm no fool. The last time we sparred I got in a lucky strike and broke his nose. Even half blind with pain, he threw me across the room. I'm really not anxious to give him a chance for some payback. I like my nuts exactly where they are."

"Wise decision. By the way, I got a call from Bryce. Seems he's having trouble with that pup you dropped off."

With a flare of alarm zinging down his spine, Mick sat up in his chair. "Rio? What's wrong?" In the face of Booth's raised brow of interest, Mick reached for his normal nonchalant attitude. "Not that it's my problem, but what's going on?"

"Let's see, how did Bryce put it? Oh yes, the kid's recalcitrant, sullen, smart-mouthed, and just plain rebellious."

Mick felt a smile tugging at his mouth. "Sounds like Rio, all right."

"Hmm, yes, well, apparently he's tried to run away twice. He was taken for a meeting with a counselor as you suggested. During the session he excused himself to go to the restroom and disappeared. He was found a couple of hours later associating with some rather unsavory characters at a certain bar, Dario's, to be precise."

"Dario's? Jesus Christ. What the fuck was he thinking? And how the hell did he get in there in the first place?"

Dario's was a popular pickup joint, one that was frequented by various paranormal species as well as humans. That Rio had found that particular bar had to be pure luck...bad luck.

"Apparently, one of the regular patrons got him in. Fortunately he was seen by a member of Bryce's pack. Bryce had put out the word for his people to be on the lookout for him. The second time he tried to leave, he snuck out in the middle of the night. What he didn't know is that Bryce had recently had an intruder spell cast to blanket his property. Has he told you Becky's expecting their first pup?"

"No. I haven't spoken to Bryce since I dropped Rio off."

"Ah, well, apparently he's not broadcasting the news yet, so keep that to yourself. Anyway, because he's feeling very protective of her, Bryce invokes the charm when they're sleeping. When Rio crossed the barrier on his way out, Bryce was woken from a sound sleep by a subcutaneous alarm. When he checked things out he found Rio missing and hauled him back before he got more than a couple of blocks away. To say he's a little disgruntled by the kid's behavior is putting it mildly."

"Fuck. I know Rio can be difficult but Bryce had better not..." Mick began harshly before cutting his sentence off midstream. The look his boss was giving him, piercing and speculative, was making him very uncomfortable.

"I know you don't really believe Bryce would hurt him," Booth said, as though knowing exactly what concerned Mick.

"I do know that," Mick conceded, and rolled his head trying to loosen the tension in his shoulders. "You need me for anything else today?"

Booth shook his head. "No, you're clear for the day."

"Great. I think I'll look Narev up after all. Might as well make somebody's day," he muttered. "Later."

"Sure," Booth answered.

* * *

A slight frown pinched the skin between Booth's brows as he watched his best enforcer walk away. Drumming his fingers on his desk, he considered an idea for a moment then picked up the phone and dialed a number. When the call was answered he spoke to the man who'd greeted him. "Bryce? It's Booth. Do me a favor. The next time your pup tries to run, let him go."

"Are you nuts? You want me to just abandon him?" Bryce growled.

"No, I'm not suggesting any such thing. What I want you to do is call Mick and let him know the kid's gone."

"What the hell for?"

"I want to test a theory."

"What theory?"

"I'd rather not say. But if it works out the way I think it will, you'll know soon enough." After being assured of Bryce's agreement, Booth disconnected the call. "Hmm. Interesting. Who'd have thought it? I'd like to meet this kid." Picking up his sandwich, Booth took a bite and went back to his paperwork.

* * *

By the time Mick got home most of the bruises had healed and the limp he'd acquired was barely noticeable. Just as he'd thought, Narev had been very pleased to see him, so pleased that he proceeded to try to rearrange Mick's anatomy by bending parts of him in directions they weren't meant to go. It had taken all of Mick's strength to remain in one piece.

If not for his werewolf physiology, he'd have been admitted to a hospital. As it was, he was still sore, though healing fast. A hot shower put the rest of his hurts to rights and he plopped down in front on the television to watch the evening news. Thoughts of Rio kept trying to intrude, but he ruthlessly squashed them.

Supper consisted of microwaved spaghetti in roasted red pepper sauce with a couple of pieces of garlic- and mozzarella-topped Texas toast. Afterward, Mick rooted out the book he'd been reading from among the clutter of newspapers on the end table by the sofa. Deeply immersed in the book, he was startled when the phone rang.

With some surprise, he noted it was after midnight. Mick picked up the handset. The caller ID let him know it was Bryce calling. Bracing for bad news, he answered. "Bryce. What's up?"

"I'll get right to the point. Your pup ran away again."

Controlling his instant annoyance and the gut-deep twang of alarm that struck, Mick replied, "First of all, he's not my pup, and second, are you looking for him?"

"I've got my people on the lookout for him, but I gotta tell you, this is getting old. I can't control him."

"Bryce, I've seen you control guys who could snap a twelve-inch diameter log in half like a twig. What is it about this kid that's so different?"

"He's afraid of me."

"So were those other guys. What the fuck did you do?" Mick growled. "If you hurt him, I swear --"

"Back down, Matranga. I didn't touch him. Goddamn, I thought you knew me better than that. You know I wouldn't use strong-arm tactics on a pup."

Taking a deep breath, Mick forced himself to squelch his runaway imagination in favor of rational thought. He rose from his seat on the sofa and began pacing around his living room. "Shit. Yeah, sorry. I do know better than that, but what do you mean he's afraid of you?"

"Maybe I should say it's not me but what I am."

"What are you talking about?"

"My alpha status. It's the only explanation I can think of. Rio seems okay with the few other members of the pack he's met. He's not exactly friendly, but he's quiescent in their company. He's wary of Becky for some reason and never lets himself be alone with her. But with me, every time I come near him I can smell his fear. He tries to hide it but it's there. Sometimes I can actually see the panic building in his eyes."

Mick listened to Bryce's reasoning for Rio's behavior and silently cursed. Rio had all but shouted his distrust of alphas; why didn't he have sense enough to listen before the kid dealt with his fear in the only manner he felt open to him?

"What the hell does he think I'm going to do to him, Mick? I know from what Booth's told me that the guy who abused him was a pack alpha. I've tried sitting him down and explaining to him that that bastard's behavior was an extreme exception and not a rule where alphas are concerned, but nothing I say is getting through. I don't know what to do with him. I can't help him if he's too scared to listen to me."

"You tried. It's not your fault Rio couldn't make himself believe you." Mick was at a loss as to what to do until something occurred to him. "So why did you call me now? From what I've heard this makes what, the third time he's run? You never called before when you were having trouble with him."

"Booth asked me to."

"*Booth*? Why?"

"He didn't say. He just said next time I have trouble with Rio to call you."

"Son of a bitch. What's he expect me to do about it?"

"I don't have a clue, but for starters you could help us look for him."

"I can do that. Have you checked Dario's again?"

"Not yet. I figured he'd be too smart to go back there since that's where we found him the first time."

"That's probably what he's counting on. I'll start there first."

"All right. Call me if you find him."

"Will do." Mick hung up and after exchanging his sweats for jeans. and, donning shoes, he was off.

Half an hour later he was parking his vehicle a couple of blocks down the street from Dario's. There was a long line of people waiting to get in. Paranormals and humans alike were dressed in trendy clothing, their attire and endless chatter making them resemble a flock of animated peacocks. Mick bypassed the line and flashed his ID at the burly bouncer. With a toothy grimace and a barely audible hiss, the weretiger waved him in. Transparent stripes appeared on the man's face and Mick felt his own invisible hackles rise. It was only the steadying influence of their human sides that kept them from mixing it up like the otherworldly cat and canine they were.

About to bypass the guy and enter the club, Mick caught a familiar scent. He leaned in and gave the man's shirt a sniff. It was definitely Rio's scent and it was fresh.

"What the fuck you doin', dog?" the bouncer snarled.

"Can the tough act, kitty. Tell me about a kid who was here or is here now." Mick described Rio. "And don't tell me you didn't see him. I can smell him on you," Mick growled while getting up in the man's face.

The bouncer's hands came up in a gesture of capitulation. "Hey, I didn't touch that sweet-assed thang. I'm not into jailbait. He brushed up against me on his way out."

"Where'd he go, with who and how long ago?"

With a jerk of his thumb, the bouncer indicated the direction. "Down the alley, two vamps, five minutes tops."

Mick was moving before the man finished speaking. Hearing that Rio was in the company of not one but two vamps set his heart to pounding. Vamps had a notorious taste for werewolf blood, and two of them could easily drain Rio. Since the inception of the CFSBE, such things were less common but not beyond the realm of possibility. It all depended on the morals of the vamps in question and Mick wasn't willing to bet Rio's life on anyone's personal sense of right and wrong.

The alley he traversed was shrouded in darkness relieved only by a couple of security lights over two side entrances to the adjacent buildings. For an alley it was relatively clean with no trash to trip the unwary, not that Mick would have stumbled over something like some amateur tracker. His senses guided him perfectly, and he moved at a rapid yet cautious pace. He had no intention of being taken by surprise or running into those he sought without getting a chance to assess the situation. With three-quarters of the narrow passage behind him, he heard voices ahead and lengthened his stride. The alley let out on a narrow access street between the backs of the businesses that populated this particular block. In the shelter between two large dumpsters stood three people.

For a split second Mick froze, stunned by the tableau before him. One of the vamps stood with his back to the wall. His arms were wound tightly around Rio holding him in place while effectively neutralizing the young man's attempts to escape. Rio was wearing a button-down shirt and jeans, both of which were open and disarranged, exposing him from neck to upper thighs. His pale skin shone in the dim light. Fully erect, his cock rose high and hard. The vamp behind him was feeding from Rio's throat while his hips thrust obscenely against Rio's bare ass.

The other vamp knelt at Rio's feet and reached for his cock. "Seed and blood. Little wolf, I'm going to suck you dry."

"No!" Rio gasped, his eyes glazing over.

As the second vamp bent his head, Mick roared and launched himself at them. His attack sent the vamp at Rio's feet crashing backward with such force that he hit the wall of the building on the opposite side of the access road and bounced like a rag doll. Surprise had the first vamp releasing his hold on Rio to defend himself. As Rio began to crumple, Mick caught him with one arm and slammed the fist of his free arm into the first vamp's face. His skull slammed into the brick wall with a resounding crack that left an impression as chunks of brick cascaded to the pavement. The surprised vamp slid down the wall to land with a dazed thump. Mick had a split second to note the closed fly on the vamp's slacks and relief flooded him. The bastard hadn't been fucking Rio but was merely dry humping him. That realization cooled Mick's blind fury, and in all probability saved the vampire's life.

A hiss sounded from behind them, and Mick whirled to face an attack. What he saw was the second vamp standing up to dust himself off, but there was no attack forthcoming.

"We weren't going to kill him, you know. Such a delectable morsel should be sampled more than once. It would have been a terrible waste to dispatch him after one taste."

"He's not yours to fucking sample," Mick growled, adrenaline and agitation making his voice a gravelly rasp.

"Then he shouldn't have been offering himself. You wolves have no manners at all. You're all so tasty, but you refuse to share. It's a damn shame," the vamp responded with sincere regret. "You really can't blame us for taking advantage of the situation. Best you keep a leash on your naive little pup before you lose him. We weren't the only ones wanting to play with him. You're lucky it was us and not the incubus that was salivating over him. That particular one has teleportation skills. You'd never have found your little boy toy before he was fucked raw and drained."

"He's not a goddamned toy and if you're expecting me to thank you, that'll happen when hell freezes over," Mick snarled. Hot rage warred against the ice that chilled his blood at the thought of Rio in the hands of an incubus. "I suggest you take your buddy and get the hell out of here before I really lose my temper."

"Tsk, tsk," the vamp answered. He cautiously sidled around Mick to help his rapidly recovering partner to his feet and the two of them disappeared down the alley.

Mick kept his gaze on them until they were out of sight, then turned his attention to Rio, who was just beginning to stir. Gently he propped the young man against the brick wall and lightly slapped his cheek. "Rio, snap out of it, kid."

Trying to keep his touch strictly impersonal, Mick started righting Rio's dislodged clothing. Now that the danger was past, the adrenaline pumping through his veins was finding a new way to ready his body. Not for a fight this time, but for sex.

Mick's cock stiffened, his body's reaction instinctive and involuntary. Heat filled his eyes as he let his gaze move slowly down Rio's body. Though slim, his muscle definition was nothing short of mouth-wateringly *fine*. Those tempting ridges practically begged to be touched. Rio's erection had diminished, but not entirely. Seeing that still plump, ivory column of flesh sent a fresh push of need straight to Mick's gut.

"*Son of a bitch*. Remind me why I keep calling you kid. That right there is definitely man-sized." He could practically feel the satiny skin that overlaid Rio's solid erection, and his fingers twitched with the need to wrap around and stroke it until it released the cream he longed to taste.

Gritting his teeth in frustration, Mick made himself pull the edges of Rio's open shirt together, which had the immediate effect of shielding that tempting body from view. Breathing hard, he rapidly did up the buttons but drew the line at restoring the kid's jeans. No way was he going to be able to tuck Rio inside them and do up the zipper. If he laid one finger on that enticing cock he was a goner.

"Shit," he growled, agitated at having to fight a battle to stay in control.

"Huh? Mick?" Dazed silver-gray eyes blinked a few times before they focused.

"Yeah, it's me. Got yourself into some trouble, didn't you?" Mick answered, glad to have the distraction.

Rio shook his head as though to clear it. "Yeah…I…uh…didn't know…vampires."

"That's right. Vampires." Mick took Rio's chin in hand and tilted it upward to examine his throat. A bit of drying blood marred its smooth expanse, but the puncture wounds had already healed. "They got a piece of you too."

"Shit. Felt like I'd been drugged."

"That's why most werewolves avoid them. We don't like not having control over our own bodies. It interferes with our natural fight-or-flight instincts. The inner wolf has a real problem with that." Rio was rapidly recovering and Mick snagged the kid's gaze. "I started putting things back together, but you might want to take care of that."

Rio followed Mick's downward glance and cursed. Staggering slightly, he pulled his jeans up, spun around, and fastened them. Mick's relieved amusement was short-lived.

Reaction to the worry he'd been dealing with since Bryce had called swept over him. When Rio turned back, Mick grabbed his shoulders and pushed him against the wall. "What the *hell* is wrong with you? Do you *not* have a brain in that head of yours? How many times do you have to be told it's dangerous out here? How much shit do you have to go through before you finally get it!?"

Wide-eyed and white-faced, Rio stared into the Mick's eyes, then dropped his gaze. "Sorry," he mumbled.

"You're sorry. Well, that fixes everything. What were you planning to do anyway? What were you going to get out of this?" Mick growled and, with a wave of his hand, broadly indicated their current situation.

"Money, all right?" Rio snarled back. Color was rapidly suffusing his cheeks. "Money so I could leave!"

"And go where!"

"I don't know! I don't fucking know! I just know I can't stay where I'm at!"

Rio attempted to push him away, but Mick crowded him hard against the wall, nudging his knee between Rio's thighs and effectively trapping him. He grabbed Rio's wrists, pushed them above his head and holding them both in one hand, made him be still. Their gazes locked. Rio's struggles abruptly stopped altogether and, as though giving permission, his chin tipped upward, his lips parting. Fire flared in Mick's veins and he gave in to that silent provocation. Lowering his mouth to Rio's, he took what was offered.

The taste that burst on his tongue as he slid it into the warm, sweet depths of Rio's mouth all but blinded him with lust. Mick ground his hips against Rio's belly and felt an answering hardness rock against his thigh. Husky moans vibrated between them and elation sang through his veins. He no longer had to imagine how Rio would sound when he was aroused. His eager cries were glorious. His body surged against Mick's as though fighting to get closer. Willing to help, Mick slid his hand between the wall and Rio's ass and, firmly cupping that taut curved mound, he pulled Rio tight against him.

The hand holding Rio's wrists imprisoned, released them. Slim arms were lowered to wrap around Mick's neck while his free hand emulated the one that already had a handful of Rio's ass. Giving that second tantalizing globe a squeeze, he slid his hand up and under Rio's shirt. Wanting the feel of skin, he was rewarded with the smooth warmth of firm flesh under his fingertips. Tracing a path up the line of his spine, Mick absorbed Rio's shiver. The moan his touch elicited made him wonder what other reactions he could provoke and, determined to find out, he began unbuttoning the shirt he had so recently restored to order.

Freeing his mouth from Rio's, Mick nuzzled and nibbled his chin, captivated by the contrast between velvety skin and the few prickly stubbles he found there. His mouth slid down the length of the vulnerable throat so trustingly bared

to him until he found the smears of dried blood left from
Rio's risky adventure with the vampires. Mick flattened his
tongue over them and moistened the red streaks until the
coppery flavor was released, absorbed and consumed. The
taste of blood ignited his wolf's response. His own teeth
reclaimed the spot his clamoring inner wolf insisted was
theirs and he bit down, not enough to break the skin but
enough to pinch the flesh, allowing him to suckle it until
more blood rose to the surface.

Rio's fingers dug into his shoulders. "Unnn, Mick, *yesss*."

Mick answered with a rumbling growl and loosed his
hold. Eyes lighting on the results of his bite, he was hit by
the pure need to possess. His wolf howled its triumph and
urged him to fully claim the young man in his arms. His
senses entangled by his wolf's demands, Mick clutched Rio's
ass in both hands and lifted.

"Wrap your legs around me," he ordered in a husky-
voiced rasp.

Rio obeyed and, pushing him flush to the wall behind
them, Mick freed his hands to part the fabric of Rio's shirt.
His vision zeroed in on two tan and tempting circles, the
backdrops for twin male nipples. Dipping his head down, he
laved his tongue over first one then the other, urging the
tiny nubs to grow hard. With lips and teeth he trapped one
beneath the suctioning of his mouth and worked it until it
swelled against his tongue. Rio cried out and bucked in his
arms, but Mick kept him pinned in place as first one nipple
then the other was treated to his sensual caresses.

Hungering for another taste of Rio's lips, Mick reached
up to cup his cheeks and brought their mouths together. His

invading tongue was boldly met by Rio's. A burst of savage delight twisted his belly and made his cock literally ache to be buried within the warmth of this brash young man's body. There was no need to wonder if Rio wanted him; the desire burning between them was most definitely mutual.

Momentarily releasing his captive's mouth, he looked into silver-gray eyes that reflected stunned surprise. Rio was clearly experiencing something unexpected and, from his physical reaction, it was by no means unpleasant. Smiling at the rush of satisfaction he experienced from Rio's response, Mick ground out in a no-nonsense tone, "You're going nowhere. Understand?"

Apparently taken in by the same wild rush Mick was experiencing, Rio nodded. "Nowhere. Got it. Kiss me again."

Only too willing to give in to that throaty-voiced demand, Mick complied. Mouths engaged, their bodies rocked together and Mick lost himself in the drugging rhythm until a sound intruded on his consciousness. His cell phone was ringing. Knowing it was probably Bryce checking in cooled his ardor. He knew he had to answer it and let those looking for Rio know he was found. Disengaging from their kiss, he huffed out an exasperated sigh against those swollen, kiss-dampened lips and released his grip on Rio. Oh so reluctantly, he urged the young man to loosen his legs and Mick steadied him as his feet again found purchase on the ground.

"I've got to take this," he said and backed away when Rio nodded. Taking his cell phone from the clip on his belt, he answered. "I found him."

"Is he all right?" Bryce immediately asked.

"Yeah. He had a run-in with a couple of vamps, but he's okay. Listen, I'm taking him home with me for tonight."

"All right, but we're going to have to come up with a better solution than the one we've got now."

"I know. We'll think of something, just not tonight. I think we need to unwind for a bit."

At Bryce's obvious concern, Mick felt a pang of guilt. His friend was thinking in terms of Rio's long-term welfare and all he wanted to do right now was to take the kid home and fuck him. What the hell was he thinking? Where had all his good intentions gone? Were a few sizzling kisses and granted, some seriously hot groping all it took to make him willing to trash all his earlier objections? No. This had to stop here and now before things went too far. With his lust rapidly draining away, Mick continued to mentally kick himself. Rio had been through enough without being casually used by someone who was supposed to protect him. Even though a part of him denied that there was nothing at all casual about what was brewing between himself and Rio, Mick chose to ignore it.

"All right. Talk to you tomorrow," Bryce agreed, drawing Mick's attention back to him.

"Sure. G'night," Mick managed in spite of his distraction. He closed his cell phone and looked over to see Rio watching him.

"I'm going home with you?" he asked.

"Yeah. For now. Um, listen, about what just happened…"

"It's okay. We both got a little carried away. Heat of the moment stuff, right?" Rio shrugged. "It's no big deal."

Relieved but wary and wondering if Rio's nonchalant attitude was for real; Mick frowned but let it go. Perhaps their mutual lapse was better ignored rather than discussed, even though he did find it a little irritating. Was Rio really as unaffected as he seemed to be? No. There was no way his passion had been faked. He'd taken every bit as much pleasure as Mick had in that ardent though imprudent interlude.

Taking a bit of perverse comfort in that realization, even as he dealt with the discomfort of a hard and unsatisfied cock, Mick motioned him to follow as he started walking. "Come on then. I'm parked a couple blocks from here."

Instead of taking the alleyway and retracing their steps, which would lead them past the club, Mick led them down the narrow access road to the end of the block then up and over two blocks to his SUV. Keying open the locks, he watched Rio climb in then went around to the driver's side where he folded himself in behind the steering wheel. Before he could start the engine, his cell phone rang. Grabbing the phone, Mick checked the caller ID, frowned and answered the call. It was his boss.

"Matranga."

"I hear you found the wandering pup."

"Yeah, I got him."

"Good. Take him home with you."

"I already am. I told Bryce we'd figure out a long-term solution tomorrow."

"Not necessary. You're it."

"*What?*"

"As of right now, you're on leave for as long as it takes to get this kid straightened around."

"Booth. What the fuck? Why me?"

"He obviously trusts you, that's why."

"Where the hell did you get that idea?"

"He talked to you, didn't he? Opened up about his problems at home? That indicates a level of trust. It's obvious by the detail you went into on your report that you care about the kid. I've never known you to make suggestions for a victim's aftercare, Mick. It's the perfect solution."

"Perfect for who?"

"For all of us who'd be inconvenienced by having to constantly chase the kid down. Or do you want to take the chance that the next time he runs something irreparable happens to him?"

Mick glanced over at Rio, who was studiously looking out the window as though trying to ignore the conversation taking place between Mick and his boss. Rio's run-in with the vamps had been bad enough, but Booth didn't know the half of it. While Mick knew he wasn't willing to risk Rio getting hurt should he run away again, there was more at stake here than just that. There was Mick's very real weakness where Rio was concerned, and it made him feel that the proper thing would be to put distance between himself and this maddening kid as soon as possible.

"No, I don't want to take that chance, but listen, there's more going on here than you know."

"Oh? Well, whatever it is, handle it."

"Jeez, Booth, if you knew what I was talking about, handling it would be the last thing you'd want me to do."

Mick could swear he heard Rio snicker and he sent a sharp glance his way, but Rio had pasted on an expression of supreme innocence and refused to meet Mick's eyes.

"You're not making any sense, Matranga."

"I'll explain if you'll shut up and listen," Mick snarled, returning his attention to his boss.

"No need for that. You've got your orders."

"Booth."

"You can thank me later."

"*For what?*" Mick could hear the smirk in Booth's voice and it grated. Why did it seem he was suddenly the butt of a joke no one had even bothered to tell him?

"Nothing specific as yet. At this point it's a working theory. Let's wait and see, shall we? Enjoy your mentorship, Mick."

Before Mick could say anything in reply, Booth hung up. He looked at the phone with a slightly bemused expression. "I'll be damned."

"What?" Rio asked.

"When you join the workforce, be sure you don't have a nosy boss who thinks he knows everything."

"Okaaay," Rio drawled with a confused frown.

Mick snickered but couldn't for the life of him figure out what was so funny. He had the feeling he was losing his grip and on top of that it seemed he was stuck playing nursemaid to someone who was temptation personified. But as precarious as the situation might be, laughter seemed a far better way to handle it rather than getting bent out of shape. "Never mind. We're going to Bryce's."

"But I thought you said…" Rio began in protest.

"Just to pack your bag," Mick explained, forestalling any argument. "Apparently you're coming home with me. At least for the next few weeks."

"Oh."

Rio's mild response made Mick smile. He had a feeling the kid was as relieved as he was. Why they both should feel that way was something he didn't want to think about, especially when moments before he'd wanted nothing more than to put space between them. Lots and lots of space. Of course, for Rio, he was probably relieved to be getting away from Bryce, but Mick had the suspicion there was more to that as well.

For all that his contradictory and confused desires and emotions were making him dizzy, this situation was damned interesting. It had been a long time since he'd had this much personal excitement in his life. He just had to make sure the balance didn't shift too far one way or the other. If it did, someone was going to get hurt. Sobering at that thought, Mick started the engine, pulled his seat belt across his chest and, snapping it shut, eased the SUV out into the street.

From the corner of his eye, Rio watched Mick maneuver the SUV into traffic then allowed himself a small, tentative smile. While things had worked out unexpectedly, this was far preferable to what he'd originally planned. Living with

Bryce and his wife had proved to be impossible. Sure they were nice, and everything seemed to be okay on the surface, but he just couldn't relax. He kept waiting for Bryce or Becky or both of them to drop their masks and plunge him into some new hell. The waiting was driving him nuts and he knew he had to leave or go crazy. He'd been plagued with nightmares, and there'd been no strong arms to hold him or familiar musky male scent to soothe away his fears.

He missed Mick. No matter how ridiculous that notion seemed or how many times he tried to talk himself out of it, the thought just wouldn't go away. It didn't seem to matter that they were practically strangers. He wanted to be with the CFSBE enforcer who had rescued him and if he couldn't, then he'd rather be alone. That it was Mick who'd shown up to save him again had seemed like a miracle. Almost as miraculous as what had happened after the vamps had been dispatched.

The vampire's bite had left him woozy and aroused. When Mick had pinned him to the wall and started yelling at him, Rio's answering anger had fueled that arousal, intensifying it to the point where he couldn't overcome the urge to defiantly offer himself to Mick. He still didn't understand why he'd felt the need to do it. Sure he'd been horny, but every sexual encounter he'd had that included a partner had been nothing but embarrassing, painful, disgusting, or terrifying. He'd truly expected to be rejected out of hand, but when Mick not only accepted but kissed him and touched him with a passion that made him feel like he was going up in flames, Rio's surprise had been absolute.

Through the windshield, he absently noted the passing traffic outside. Neon signs and headlights illuminated the busy street. Inside the vehicle, separated from that visible rush of activity, Rio sought to unravel the confusion of his feelings versus what had happened between him and Mick.

For Rio, sex had become a complicated, confusing and mostly painful issue. His sexual encounters with his stepmother had brought fear and guilt along with pleasure. The sex he had with strangers for money was as impersonal as he could make it. It had been nothing more than providing a service while keeping himself as distanced from it as possible, even if that distance existed only in his mind. Those encounters were fraught with disgust, resignation, and self-castigation. With Sutter, sex had entailed fear and pain. If he didn't perform as expected, Sutter made him suffer. The fear and pressure he'd been under made it impossible for him to feel anything but loathing for the sexual acts he'd been forced to endure.

How had something that could be so pleasurably explosive turned into something so completely dismal? Like any young and healthy being, he'd followed his natural physical urges and masturbated. He more than enjoyed the act. Like everyone else, he expected sex would be even better, but he had learned the hard way that the act itself wasn't what truly mattered. It was the partner you chose to indulge with. Sex with the wrong person could be like a glimpse into hell.

Rio chanced a quick glance to where Mick sat confidently steering the vehicle in which they rode through the late-night traffic. A thrill of desire twisted his stomach.

When Mick kissed him in that alley, he'd been utterly stunned. He'd never had anything that even remotely compared to what Mick had given him. It had been heat and need and lust for sure, but also safety and something else. Something so out of the realm of his experience that he couldn't even begin to put a name to it. He wasn't sure what would have happened had Mick not received that call, but he had a feeling he would have agreed to just about anything. When Mick touched him, it felt good and right, not terrifying, tawdry, or demeaning.

Of course, the phone call had put the lid on that. As Mick had talked to Bryce, Rio could actually see the change come over him. His body language had gone from unconsciously fluid and sensual to tense and uneasy. When the call ended and those penetrating blue-green eyes had focused on him once again, Rio knew that things had changed again. That's why he'd so rapidly offered Mick a more than plausible out. He didn't want Mick to change his mind about letting him go home with him. If it meant pretending that what had happened between them was no big deal, then he'd pretend his ass off. No matter how much it hurt. And it had hurt.

Having all that forceful, down and dirty yet strangely cleansing passion turn cool had stung. Losing that feeling of security he had been given when Mick held him had left Rio feeling adrift. Maybe Mick would never really want him, but if he could at least stay close to him, things might not be so bad.

That second phone call had been the best thing that had happened to him since the night Mick had rescued him.

Though he tried not to eavesdrop, it was kind of hard the way his senses had been getting sharper and sharper. He'd wanted to cheer when Mick's boss gave him over into Mick's care. And hadn't that just about panicked Mick? His attitude kind of pissed Rio off, but on some level he understood why Mick felt that way. He relaxed fingers that had tightened into fists, flattened one hand against his thigh and thoughtfully fingered the seat belt stretched across his chest with the other.

He was pretty sure it had something to do with those things Mick had said about Rio trying to protect his dad. He implied that it should have been his dad protecting him. Rio figured Mick felt that things between them should be the same way, with Mick protecting him, not fucking him. Mick obviously thought of him as a kid. Look at how many times he actually called him "kid" instead of by name.

Well, Rio had news for him. He might be close to a kid in years but he didn't feel like one anymore. He'd seen too many things and done more of them than he wanted. Maybe that was another reason Mick withdrew from him. He wasn't exactly pure anymore, and did Mick even do guys? He'd been married to a woman, so what did that mean? Still, that kiss hadn't been a figment of his imagination. Mick had wanted him. At least for those few wild and unguarded moments.

With his thoughts jumping around and going in circles, Rio finally heaved an exasperated sigh. It was exhausting having everything up in the air. There was the werewolf thing to deal with, which scared him more than the nightmares he'd been having. Now there was this unexpected and confusing need for Mick. A few days ago Rio would have sworn he'd never need anybody, but something deep inside was proving him wrong. It was almost as though there was another entity inside him, something that was, but was not, part of him all at the same time. It was that unknown entity that seemed to be steering him in Mick's direction.

An inkling of an idea tickled his brain. "Mick?"

"Yeah."

"What's it like to be a werewolf? I mean inside."

"I'm not sure what you mean."

Rio intercepted Mick's quick glance. "When you change you become a wolf, right? Four legs and all?"

"Yeah."

"So does your mind, like, become a wolf's mind, or do you still know who you are?"

"Ah. I see what you're getting at. No, you don't lose yourself. It's almost like there are two minds and two spirits inhabiting your body. Whichever form you take has the dominant position. As a human, your human habits, instincts, morals, et cetera, rule you. When you take your wolf form, it's the wolf who rules. But the good thing about it is that it's not absolute either way."

"Huh?"

"Each mind is aware of the other. The wolf can influence the human and the human can influence the wolf."

"I see. So each is aware of the other no matter what form you're in?"

"That's right." Mick glanced at him again before turning his attention back to the road. "Rio, are you beginning to sense your wolf?"

"I think so."

"I thought you might."

"What made you think that?"

"You've done a few things that were rather wolfy. Normally you don't become aware of it until after the change. I think in your case, even though the actual physical change was prevented, some of the other components managed to slip through. The development of your wolf, for one. Your senses have improved, haven't they? Hearing, scent and the rest?"

"Yeah."

"That explains why you laughed when I was talking to Booth."

Rio dropped his chin. "Sorry. I couldn't help hearing what you guys were saying."

Mick sighed. "It's all right. No harm done. You know I'm really not all that reluctant to have you with me. I want you to know that. I just think we need to be careful about getting carried away in certain areas. You understand?"

Rio felt his heart contract with an unexpected jolt of pain. Once more that "other" part was expressing itself, and it wasn't happy, but Rio overruled it. He was still human. He was in charge, at least for now, and for now, to stay close to Mick, this was the way it had to be.

"I understand." With that settled, Rio let his mind drift back over the events of the evening. He was suddenly struck by an incredulous realization. "Mick?"

"Yeah?"

"Did two vampires really try to eat me tonight?"

"Yeah."

"Holy shit."

"Holy shit indeed."

* * *

Mick provided Rio with his own bedroom, one of two contained in the house he owned. Wanting to live in a more rural setting, Mick had sold the condo he'd shared with his wife and bought five acres of former farmland that was located on a quiet country road. His house was actually a sturdy renovated building that was once used to house farm equipment. He'd examined the building when considering his purchase of the land and decided he liked the weathered wood on the outside and the thick beams and rough-hewn support columns on the inside. It had taken a lot of work to make it habitable; the plumbing and electrical work alone had been a nightmare, but it had been worth it.

The building had been insulated and reinforced with new inner walls. It was then divided up into several rooms. At one end of the house was the kitchen, partitioned off from the combination living room and dining room by open counters. From the living room a hallway marched down the center of the living space to the other end of the house. On one side of it was a large walk-in closet, a small bathroom with toilet, sink and shower stall only, and finally a midsize bedroom. The other side had a small room, which Mick used for storage with the rest of the space being taken up by the master suite which came complete with Jacuzzi, an item Mick rarely used. He preferred the large shower stall with its multiple showerheads.

There was a smaller building catty-corner from the house where he stored lawnmowers, tools and a few other things. He was also in the process of building a garage. The house sat nearly dead center of the property and the rest of the land was open lawn, planted with a multitude of sheltering trees.

There were only four other residences on the mile-wide block, which suited him perfectly. He'd met two of the neighbors while retrieving his mail from the mailbox near his driveway. They liked to walk the length of the road for exercise during good weather and hellos had been exchanged when they passed by. A third neighbor was met because of a little dog that had taken an unreasonable fascination with him. He had to return the fawning little shit of a terrier to his elderly owner at least once a month except during the winter months when snow kept Binky trapped at home.

After the first night Rio stayed, Mick wasted no time in setting up a routine for him. The sessions with his counselor were reinstated, and Rio was enrolled in online classes so that he could earn his GED since he'd run away before graduating. Mick also kept him busy with the construction being done on the garage as well as yard work.

"You ever do this kind of thing before?" Mick asked him while preparing his riding mower for a session of work.

"Mow the lawn? Well, duh, yeah," Rio replied. "That was part of my chores at home. Do I get to run the riding mower?"

"Nope. I've got something much better in mind for you." Mick struggled to hide his smile at the sight of Rio's suspiciously furrowed brow.

"What?"

"You get to use the push mower to trim around the trees."

"Oh *man*." Rio looked out over the land around them, his eyes squinting in the midmorning sunlight. "There's so many of them."

"Yeah. Nice, huh? Tell you what. You do half and we'll switch places. It's not gonna be that big a chore, and we don't have to do the entire thing in one day. Besides that, the mower's self-propelled. It'll be like a walk in the park, no pun intended."

"Ha ha," Rio answered as Mick's property did indeed resemble a park in many ways.

"Before you get started, go in the house and put on some sunblock. It's on the kitchen table. With that pale skin of yours you'll be redder than a beet in no time. Just because the body heals fast is no reason to abuse it unnecessarily. I left you a pair of goggles too. They're tinted so they'll help with the glare and protect your eyes. Later you might think about making a list of things you need or would like to have, like sunglasses," Mick suggested while adjusting his own shades. "We can do some shopping in a day or two."

"All right," Rio agreed.

Mick watched Rio walk away and sighed. The first day of the full moon was coming. Two weeks from now, hence his strong desire to keep Rio busy. The less time he had to think about it, the better. If wearing Rio out with yard work would help to keep him from worrying more than need be, Mick was all for it. He had some ideas about how to make the first shift easier for Rio, but he wasn't sure if he should employ them. The things he had in mind could come back to bite him on the ass.

It wasn't unusual -- and in fact was an accepted practice -- for an older, experienced were to be assigned the task of helping a human turned were, through his or her first shift. For born weres, when they shifted at puberty, their bodies had the advantage of knowing and beginning the change by slow degrees on a cellular level months before the actual change. So, while the process was painful it was not debilitating, and thus they were left to handle it on their own. Not so for the turned human. Their first transformation was an abrupt and shocking alteration with death or madness a very real possibility.

Part of the method employed to help alleviate the pain of the shift for a bitten human was to use sex. The pleasure detracted from the pain as well as distracted the first time human shifter so that the transformation could take place as smoothly and as swiftly as possible. Mick was still debating with himself about talking to Rio about it when the young man returned.

Mick figured he still had time to think about it although he really didn't see any other option that would be of any greater help in getting Rio through the coming ordeal.

Putting his thoughts aside in favor of getting to work, he got Rio started then climbed on the riding mower and concentrated on doing the job. A couple of hours later, he traded places with the kid.

"Keep one thing in mind," he warned him as the eager young man climbed aboard and settled into the riding mower's seat. "This is not a freaking Indy car. You're not breaking any speed records and the first time you bounce off one of the trees you're back to push mower duty. Got it?"

"Got it," Rio agreed with a grin.

Mick snorted. "Get to work, whelp."

After watching for a few minutes to make sure Rio had the hang of running the riding mower, Mick began his stint with the push mower. Two hours later he called a halt for the day. It was late afternoon and he was starving. The idea struck him that it was a great day for cooking out, so he dragged his charcoal grill out of the tool shed. He handed Rio a bucket and the wire grate that would hold the food over the coals.

"Take this bucket in the house, fill it with hot water, and squirt some dish soap in it too. There's a grill scrubby thingy under the sink. Bring it back out here and clean the grate, would you?"

"*Scrubby thingy?*" Rio asked doubtfully, though he was smiling.

"Fuck, I don't know what you call it. It's this really tough pad with a handle. You'll find it. It's in a plastic tray with some other brushes and steel wool."

Rio did find it and finished his part of the preparations while Mick piled charcoal in the grill, doused it with starter fluid and threw a match on it. A flashing whoosh of flame engulfed the charcoal, but it eventually died down to a sullen glow that began turning the charcoal ashy around the edges.

"I've got some steak and chicken breasts in the freezer I'll defrost in the microwave to throw on here. You want hot dogs too?" Mick asked.

"Sure. I love hot dogs done on the grill."

"Me too. While I get stuff started, why don't you go clean up; then you can keep an eye on the grill while I shower."

"I can do that," Rio agreed and started into the house.

Mick stopped him. "Hey, shake the grass and shit off your clothes and out of your hair first."

"Yes, mother," Rio grouched. "Anybody ever tell you you're awfully bossy?"

"Not that I recall, but then I've never had anyone so aptly suited to be bossed staying with me." Rio made a rude sound with his lips that made Mick grin, but Rio did as he was told.

* * *

"How are you doing?" Mick stopped near the dining table on his way outside. Rio had set up the laptop the CFSBE had provided him with there and was working on his daily GED lessons.

"Okay. It's not all that hard. Once I got going a lot of stuff started coming back to me. It's mostly just a matter of slogging through it," Rio answered, glancing up from the screen.

"Well, that's good. I don't know if I'd be of much help where homework's concerned."

"You'd probably do all right. You don't seem like a complete dummy."

"Thanks a lot. I can't tell you how much your praise means to me." His mildly sarcastic reply earned him a grin from Rio, and he couldn't help but return the gesture.

Rio's happiness was infectious, and Mick was glad to see it. There'd been several incidents of late night nightmares when Rio had first moved in, but they'd diminished. He confessed they'd been a nightly occurrence while staying with Bryce and Becky. Either he felt more secure staying with Mick, or the counseling sessions he was attending were helping.

Reminded by that thought, Mick passed it on to Rio. "Don't forget you have an appointment this afternoon. Four o'clock, isn't it?"

"Yeah, I know," Rio glumly answered.

His attitude piqued Mick's curiosity. He'd made it a point not to question Rio about his sessions with Dr. Spence, but that sulky reply prompted him to ask, "Are you having a problem of some kind?"

"Not really. It's just..." He sat back in his chair and drummed his fingers on the table. "Dr. Spence makes me think about stuff."

Mick smiled. "Well, that's the idea, isn't it? You've had a lot of shit to deal with in the past couple of years. I would think talking about it, maybe hashing it out would give you a better perspective on things. Sort of help you get it off your chest and make you feel better."

"Yeah it does, but we don't just talk about the things that have happened to me. Dr. Spence makes me question other stuff."

"Like what? Shit, no, strike that. Look, I told myself I wouldn't pry into your personal life. Like I said before, I'm no psychiatrist and it's really none of my business. You can tell me if you want, but if not, don't feel you have to."

"I know," Rio assured him. He set his silver-gray eyed gaze on Mick. "But...I'd kinda like to run something by you if you don't mind."

Mick pulled out a chair and sat down. "I don't mind. Shoot."

Rio shifted his gaze out the window. "Dr. Spence asked me if I'd ever thought about whether I was straight or gay. I mean, you know, I had sex with the stepmother from hell and even though the circumstances sucked, I still got off with her. Then when I ran away, it was all stuff with guys."

"Yeah, but that's easy to explain. It's rare to see a woman out cruising for sex, I mean, you know, willing to pay for it, so it's only natural your clients, for lack of a better word, would be men."

"Yeah, that's what I told him, and he asked me if I'd ever really thought about whether I'd prefer to have sex with a woman or a man."

"Have you?"

"Well, yeah. I mean I fantasized about having sex with girls when I first started thinking about those kinds of things. I mean, we're kind of conditioned while we're growing up to think about the opposite sex, right?"

"Yeah, that's true."

"But you know, when I was having sex with guys even though I hated it, the more I think about it, the more I realize it was just because of the circumstances. The whole thing, the sex for money, the back alley crap, it all just made me feel like shit. I don't think it was because it was sex with guys. I especially realized that after what happened with you 'cause I really didn't hate that at all," Rio said in a rush. "What I think is that maybe it doesn't matter if it's a guy or a girl, it just depends on who you're with."

"I think you're absolutely right," Mick told him, secretly pleased that Rio was not only willing to admit that he'd liked what happened between them but that it hadn't had an adverse effect on him. "I've been with both sexes and it was pleasurable either way. I think that's hard for a lot of people to accept but really, when it comes to sex and maybe especially love, the gender of the two people involved should take a backseat to how they feel about each other. I don't think it would be right for love to be thrown away just because the stuffed shirts of the world don't think it's right for two women or two men to love each other."

"Yeah, exactly. I'm not sure Dr. Spence gets that."

"He's not trying to tell you what you feel is wrong, is he?"

"No, not exactly. He just seems to have a little trouble believing that I feel that way. I think he thinks maybe I'm confused by all the crap I've been through."

Mick was shocked to see Rio's eyes develop a swimming sheen as tears formed.

"But even though I've been through a lot, I'm not mental or anything. I don't feel like I'm gonna fall apart or go crazy. I have nightmares sometimes about Sutter. You know that, but I…I know what I know. You know? I'm not confused about the way I feel."

Rio turned a look of such intensity on Mick that he felt his chest seize as the air in his lungs refused to move. Rio seemed to be making a confession of sorts. For a moment Mick wasn't sure what to say or do until lack of oxygen had him taking a deep breath. It felt as though a minefield had appeared in front of him, and he had to step very carefully or be blown away.

"If you're sure of how you feel then stick to your guns," Mick finally told him. There was no way he was going to lie to Rio even if the things he was saying might put him in a precarious situation. "Don't let anyone try to change you. You have to be true to yourself. If you're not, nothing in your life will make sense. It will all be distorted because your basic beliefs are being violated."

Rio nodded and smiled. "Thanks. I won't let Dr. Spence shake me."

"Good. So are you okay with still seeing him? Do you feel like he's helping you at all?"

"Yeah, kinda. Like you said, it's good to talk about stuff. It helps me to see things a little more clearly. There's some things I need to think about, like maybe seeing my dad again."

"Do you want to?"

"Yeah. I'm not ready to face him yet but…yeah, I want to. Someday."

"I'm betting he'll be happy to see you."

"You think so?"

"Yeah, I do."

"Maybe you're right. Hey, who's that?"

Mick followed the direction of Rio's gaze and saw a red pickup truck approaching the house by way of his long, gravel-strewn driveway. "Ah, that's my brother, Jed. He's helping me build the garage."

"Your *brother*?"

"Yeah, is there something wrong with that?"

"No, I'm just surprised is all. I didn't know you had a brother."

"There's a lot you don't know about me. I've got a sister too."

"I guess you're a pretty normal guy, huh?"

Mick snorted. "Aside from being a werewolf and a CFSBE enforcer? Yeah, I guess I'm pretty normal."

"So are you gonna let me help you guys?"

"Do you want to?"

"Yeah, besides, you're the one who's been trying to keep me busy."

Mick's brow rose. "You saw through that little maneuver, huh?"

"Yeah, but it's okay. I don't want to sit around twiddling my thumbs. It makes me feel better to be doing something," Rio confessed.

"Finish up what you're doing there, and I'll set you up with a hammer and some nails," Mick replied. He rose from his chair and gave Rio a reassuring pat on the shoulder.

"Cool. It'd be even better if you had a nail gun."

"Sorry to disappoint, but we'll be sticking to the old-fashioned method here."

"Too bad. I've wanted to try one of those ever since I saw that *Lethal Weapon* movie."

"Oh yeah," Mick said with a grin. "That was cool when Murtaugh got that guy with the nail gun. Nailed him," he and Rio said in unison then laughed. "Get your stuff done and come on out. I'll introduce you to Jed."

"Okay. I won't be much longer."

He left Rio to his studies and went out to meet his brother. The two of them got started and half an hour later when Rio joined them, Mick made the introductions.

"Rio, this is my brother, Jed Matranga. Jed, Rio Hardin; he's staying with me for a while."

"How ya doin', Rio? I actually heard about you before I got here."

"Oh?" Rio and Mick asked, parroting each other.

Jed looked from one to the other and grinned. "I got a call from Mom this morning. Seems she's been talking to Becky Mills and Becky told her about how Rio's staying with you. Mom wanted to know if I knew anything about it. I told her I didn't and, fair warning, she said she was going to call you. I take it you haven't heard from her yet?"

"No, not a peep," Mick confessed.

"I imagine it won't be long before you do."

"So what exactly did Becky say to Mom? About Rio, that is."

"Just that you helped him out of a jam when you were on assignment and that he was staying with you for a while."

"Oh, I see." Mick glanced at Rio and saw the relief in his eyes. Mick didn't believe Becky would go blurting his circumstances to anyone, but the question needed to be asked just to put both his and Rio's minds at rest. "Well, come on, enough chitchat. Daylight's burning and Rio's got an appointment in town in" -- Mick looked at his watch -- "six and a half hours. I want to get some work out of him before we have to leave."

"I'm ready. We working the drywall today too?" asked Jed.

"That's right. You and Rio can nail the rest of the sheets up, and I'll start plastering over the nail indentations and tape the seams."

"Works for me. Come on Rio, let's get started," Jed said and, taking charge of Rio, the two of them got started.

As the sun rose it got warmer outside and all three of them ended up stripping off their T-shirts. Mick couldn't help casting a few surreptitious glances in Rio's direction to admire his young charge's physique and in doing so noticed that Rio was doing the same. Despite feeling not only sexually charged but frustrated in the bargain, he perversely found the whole situation funny. Perhaps if his brother hadn't been there to buffer the temptation he wouldn't have been quite so amused. At least this way he didn't have to fight with himself against making a move, which allowed him the luxury of being entertained rather than pissed.

Wiping at a trickle of sweat that tickled his temple, Mick laid aside his putty knife and went to see how Rio and Jed were doing. The two of them were industriously hammering away and when the latest piece of drywall was secure he interrupted them.

"I'm taking a bathroom break and getting some water. You guys want some?"

"Yeah," Rio answered, pushing sweaty bangs back from his forehead.

"Got beer?" Jed asked.

"Yeah, but you're not getting any. You'll end up nailing your thumb to the wall."

"Whatever you say, bro. Bring me the water. Rio and I are gonna take a breather."

"All right. I'll be back in a few minutes," Mick answered.


Rio and Jed settled on the grass in the shade cast by the garage.

"So, how long are you gonna be staying with Mick?" Jed asked.

Rio idly plucked a grass stem and looked at him. Mick and his brother did resemble each other. Their hair color was similar, though Jed's was maybe a shade or two lighter. Jed's eyes were definitely blue rather than the blue-green that

Mick's were. Jed looked to be the younger of the two and was a bit slimmer, but not by much. Rio dropped his gaze to his hands and carefully laid the grass stem between his thumbs. He blew against it, smiling when he got it to whistle.

"I don't really know how long I'll be staying here. I was, uh, bitten by a guy and turned. I haven't been through my first change yet, and Mick's going to help me."

Jed whistled. "Whoa. It's a good thing you like him."

"Huh? What are you talking about?"

"Mick. You like him, right? Can't say as I blame you. Even I can see he's a good-looking guy."

"You got a brother complex or something?"

Jed laughed. "Hell, no. I generally prefer girls, although I think I could be persuaded to try a guy if I found one as cute as you."

"Fuck. Why do people keep saying I'm cute?"

"Maybe 'cause it's true?"

"Jeez."

"Anyway, back to my original question. You like him, right? It's obvious he likes you."

"It is?"

"Sure. But he'll probably never make a move on you."

"Why?"

Jed gave Rio the once-over. "How old are you, sixteen, seventeen?"

"I'll be nineteen in about a week," Rio answered, thoroughly offended.

"Really? Nineteen, huh? Still, you're kinda young for Mick."

"He can't be that old."

"He's forty-seven."

"*What? No way!* There's no way he's a day over twenty-five, if that."

"Oh yeah, *way.* It's the werewolf thing. Didn't anyone tell you that's part of it? We age very slowly and our life spans are way longer than humans."

"How much longer?"

"At least triple, sometimes longer. But anyway, to Mick you're like a kid. He'd probably feel like he was robbing the cradle if he tried anything with you."

"Shit. I figured that was part of it."

"Part of it?"

Rio bit his lip and debated a bit before adding, "There's been some other shit that's happened to me. It started with an overly horny stepmother when I was fourteen and ended with the guy who bit me and kept me prisoner for a month. Guess you could say I was used and abused." Rio spoke in a flippant manner to hide his true feelings of pain and anger. "At any rate, I'm pretty sure Mick wouldn't want me because of it."

"Whoa, now wait a minute. Wouldn't want you? Don't kid yourself, kid. He wants you, all right. Even after being around you two for just a couple of hours, that's plain to see. Hell, I can smell it. If you're thinking Mick's looking at you like you're damaged goods, you got it all wrong. His thought processes don't work like that. If he doesn't make a move it's because he feels it would be a dishonorable thing to do." Jed leaned back on his hands and looked up at the sky. "I will tell you one thing. If you really want him, you're gonna have to make the first move. I know my brother. I've seen how he's become over the last couple of years since Maddy died. He goes out of his way to avoid serious entanglements. Her death did a number on him, and he's running scared of being with anyone again."

"You think so?"

"Heh, I know so. You know why our mother called me when she heard Mick had someone staying with him? She was hoping I'd tell her he had a lover. Our parents have been worried about him. All he does is work and play poker once a month with me and few guys. He doesn't socialize anymore. Just holes himself up here at home during his time off."

"Your parents wouldn't care if his lover was a guy?"

"Hell no. That's another thing you'll learn about werewolves. We're way more understanding about same-sex relationships. For us it's not about gender. It's about instinct. When you find your mate it doesn't matter who it is, your wolf says so and you don't get the option to refuse."

"Hmm. But…"

Before Rio could say more, Mick returned with cold bottles of water and handed them out. "You guys ready to go back to work?"

Rio and Jed got to their feet.

"I am," Jed said.

"Me too," Rio added.

"Good. We can put in another hour before lunch and a couple more hours after that before we need to stop and get ready for Rio's appointment."

Mick led the way back into the garage and Jed nudged Rio before they followed him in. "Remember what I said. You'll have to make the first move."

Rio calmly nodded even though his stomach was doing a backflip.

The work continued until Mick called the final halt for the day. Before he left to take his shower, Rio got a grin and a wink from Jed that made him laugh. Mick was giving them both suspicious looks and Rio quickly ducked out to avoid any questions. He heard Mick talking to Jed as he walked away, but he was positive Jed wouldn't spill the beans concerning what they'd talked about. Rio was pretty sure he wouldn't want to deal with a pissed-off Mick.

Once in town, Mick killed time by dropping in on Bryce and Becky while Rio did his ninety-minute stint with Dr. Spence. Afterward, the two of them did some shopping at the huge local home improvement warehouse where Mick bought an automatic garage door opener. They then had supper at a seafood restaurant where Rio got his first taste of lobster with his surf and turf platter, and the evening was topped off by grocery shopping.

Arriving home, Rio took the opportunity to put Jed's advice to work. Feeling a little awkward, being not exactly well-versed in the art of seduction, he started the ball rolling by "accidentally" brushing up against Mick as they put the groceries away. His plan worked a little too well when, with a sideways shift that went a little too far, they bumped into each other and Mick had to reach out to steady Rio as he lost his balance.

Face-to-face, Rio looked up to find Mick staring at him. "What are you doing?" Mick asked. His expression was stern, but his eyes were filled with a kind of suspicious amusement that had Rio bristling.

"Nothing. I just bumped into you. So I'm clumsy. What of it?"

"I'd say nothing, but that last maneuver was a little too obvious. Rio…are you trying to make a move on me?"

Instantly scarlet with embarrassment, Rio forcefully denied it. "Hell no! Why would you think that?"

"Hmm, well, it just seemed like it." Mick backed Rio up until his back connected with the countertop. "Remember what I told you about us having to be careful about getting carried away in certain areas?"

"I remember." Rio stood still and closed his eyes when Mick leaned forward and pressed a kiss to his forehead.

With the warmth of Mick's body so near and that distinctive scent inundating his senses, Rio was caught between arousal and another part of himself that was simply sighing at the welcomed feeling of safety and security that was flowing over him. Pure happiness and satisfaction began to wrap themselves around him like a comforting blanket when Mick's next words tore those emotions to shreds.

"You're a sweet kid, but I can't get involved with you. Okay?"

Immediately hurt, Rio pushed Mick away. "You're a jackass, you know that? I'm not a kid, and I'm not sweet. I may not know anything about relationships, but I know everything there is to know about fucking, 'cause like it or not, I've done it so it's too late to protect me. If you don't like me, just say so!"

"If I didn't like you you'd know it, and you may not think you need protection but you do. I'm not having this conversation with you, Rio, and I'm not taking you to bed either, no matter how much you think you know. End of story," Mick growled.

"Fine! Who wants you anyway?" Rio shouted.

He stomped out of the kitchen, down the hall and entered his bedroom, slamming the door behind him. Throwing himself down on his bed, Rio thought for a moment, squirmed with embarrassment then grabbed a pillow and held it down over his head until he had to let it go to breathe.

From under the sheltering fabric of the pillowcase he murmured, "Son of a bitch. That sure the hell went well."

* * *

The ensuing days passed with Mick and Rio being cautiously polite to each other. Jed continued to come to the house on a near-daily basis to help on the garage, and his presence served as a buffer between them. With Jed engaging them both in conversation and telling jokes to make them laugh, they were able to relax a bit more, and the tension between them eventually eased.

From the moment he'd met Jed, Rio liked him. His good opinion was reinforced as he got to know Mick's brother better, especially when Jed showed his concern for the problem that had developed between Mick and him. When he asked Rio about it, he swallowed his embarrassment and made a full disclosure of his clumsy seduction routine. Mick was making a quick trip into town for shingles and nails and was bringing fast food home for lunch as well, giving them the opportunity to talk freely.

Hearing his explanation, Jed laughed and clapped him on the shoulder. "You get points for trying, anyway. Don't give up. Mick is stubborn as hell, but he still wants you."

"How can you tell that? He doesn't look at me much anymore."

Jed tapped his nose. "The nose knows. He's horny as hell and it ain't me he's lusting after. At least it better not be."

That news cheered Rio considerably and, with more hope in his heart than he'd had in days, he went back to work.

# Chapter Four

Much as they both wished it could be avoided, the first night of the full moon inevitably rolled around and Mick decided it was time to discuss a few things. He baldly started the conversation with, "You've been masturbating more lately."

Rio, who'd just taken a swallow of orange juice, barely managed to gulp it down and immediately started coughing. "Fuck, that hurt! What the hell? Why did you say that?"

"Probably because it's true. You're not the only one, you know. Tonight's the night you'll shift. You've been feeling it for the past couple of days, haven't you? That restless feeling, that electric tingle under your skin?"

"Yeah, I have but...what about the other thing you said?"

Mick had to smile at the flush that colored Rio's cheeks. "The coming of the full moon affects your libido. You start feeling the need for release even more intensely and more often than usual. Thus, unless you have someone to have sex with, you masturbate more."

"Jeez, would you quit saying that?"

"Would you be more comfortable with the term jack off?"

"I'd be more comfortable if you'd shut up. Why are you telling me this?"

"Because it's a chance to make things easier tonight."

"How?"

"If you're sexually aroused and engaged in getting off, your body will be less tense. With your mind and body distracted by pleasure, the pain won't be as intense. It'll still be there, but it will blend with the pleasure, which will allow the shift to happen more rapidly."

"So what exactly is your point?"

"I want you to know what to expect, and I'm offering you an option."

"To do what?" Rio cautiously asked.

"To allow yourself to be distracted."

Rio's eyes squeezed shut. His hand went to his forehead; his fingers rubbed at the creases there. "Jesus Christ, this sucks."

"I take it that's a no."

"No, it's not a fucking no, but damn, it's like having a clinical discussion over whether or not you should fuck me. I thought you said you'd never touch me," Rio shot back, his eyes snapping open to reveal a silver-gray glitter of agitation.

"I wasn't planning on fucking you, and it wouldn't be me anyway."

"*No?*"

"No. It would be Jed." Mick winced inside at the shocked hurt he could plainly see on Rio's face.

"*What?* Are you fucking kidding me?"

"No, and like I said, it wouldn't be fucking. I think a little mutual masturbation would do the trick."

"You...you're serious."

"Look, it's not a big deal. It's an accepted practice among weres to do this kind of thing to help a newbie human through their first shift and it's not like Jed's a stranger. The two of you have gotten to know each other. You seem to like him well enough, don't you?"

"Yeah, I like Jed, but...you're okay with it? I mean with it being Jed?"

"Sure. He knows what to do. He'll help you and treat you right."

Even as he said the words, Mick's wolf was snarling and his human self wasn't hanging on to his composure by much more than a thread. The thought of anyone, even his brother whom he trusted and loved, touching Rio in that way made him want to wreak havoc on anyone and anything in his path. He knew if Rio agreed, he was going to have to put a lot of miles between his brother, Rio and himself, or risk damaging someone or something. Then again, leaving Rio, especially under those circumstances, might prove to be impossible ,which could turn out to be even more dangerous.

"I don't know whether to be pissed or to think this is funny," Rio practically growled.

"There's no reason to get upset about it."

"I'm not upset. What's there to be upset about? It's nothing personal, right? We're just talking about me and Jed jacking each other off to help me get through tonight. Fine. Whatever. I'm going for a walk."

"Rio. It's not exactly like that. I didn't mean…"

"I really don't want to talk about this anymore. I get it, okay?"

"Okay."

Hearing the sound of the front door slamming, Mick knew he'd blown it. He'd been too detached. He had the feeling that Rio had come to a very wrong conclusion. God, if Rio only knew how much this was killing him, but this was for the best. Wasn't it? And if that was so, why did he feel like punching a hole in the wall? It made him wonder just who he was trying to protect more. Rio or himself.

"Stupid fucking bastard. That son of a bitch. He's just gonna hand me over to Jed like I'm…like I'm…" At the far side of a big oak tree as far from the house as he could get, Rio dropped down to the ground and sat staring across the wide open fields. "Like I'm nothing," he whispered.

Bleak, raw pain filled his chest and made his stomach churn until, levering himself up on his knees, he vomited the breakfast he'd just eaten. Spitting to clear the sour taste from his mouth, Rio stood, staggered a few paces away and lowered himself back to the ground. Dashing involuntary tears from his eyes, he waited for the shaking to stop.

The rest of the day went by at a crawl. Mick tried to keep them both busy with yard work, which included bracing the trunk of a very large and very old maple tree near the house. Some twelve feet from the ground, the trunk, instead of being one solid mass, split into two separate and nearly identical twin trunks that branched outward in a V-shape. After a particularly bad ice storm last winter, Mick had worried that the weight of the ice would cause the tree to split right down the middle. He had decided to use heavy chain encased in very thick, flexible plastic along with a pulley system to prevent that from happening.

After getting himself and Rio into the tree by way of a ladder, each of them took one side and wrapped the chain into place. Mick affixed the pulley between the two sides and ratcheted it firmly into place. While it sounded like a simple enough thing to do, there had been some problems along the way. Rio, apparently still disgruntled from their earlier talk, had bitched and sniped at him until Mick was gritting his teeth to keep from roaring at him.

By the time the job was done, he was drenched with sweat, brittle with tension, and ready to snap. A throbbing headache beat behind his eyes and he was within inches of giving Rio the chewing out of his life. Mick settled for turning on the hose and drenching himself with ice-cold well water. The freezing jolt of it took his breath away and more than distracted him from his ire.

"What the hell are you doing?" Rio snapped, having followed on his heels like a yapping puppy.

"Keeping myself from beating you," Mick growled. Though his temper was cooling along with his body temperature, that sulky scowl on Rio's face was doing a number on him.

"What did I do?"

"What did you do?" Were those plump, ripe lips actually pouting? Mick silently swore and directed the cold water straight to his overheating groin, which made him jump and cuss out loud. "Fuck! I swear if I had to listen to you bitch one more minute I would have thrown myself out of that tree. A trip to the hospital with a broken leg would have been less painful."

"Well, excuse me for not being Mr. Lumberjack Tree-fixer Man. Why the hell I had to climb a fucking tree and do all that shit is beyond me. If the tree's gonna break, I say let it break."

"Shut. The. Fuck. Up," Mick snarled, emphasizing each word.

"Why should I? I --"

Having had enough, Mick did the only thing he could. He turned the hose on Rio.

Sputtering with surprise, Rio wiped the water out of his eyes. "You bastard. You did not just do that."

"No? Are you sure?" So saying, Mick aimed another shot at him.

With a wordless cry, Rio attacked.

Mick dodged but managed to keep the hose aimed at Rio. Determined, Rio kept coming and finally succeeded in tackling Mick around the knees but only after he'd become entangled in the hose. The two of them went down and hit the grass with a wet, squelching thump then rolled around fighting for control of the water. At first Rio settled for trying to loosen Mick's grasp on the hose by prying at his fingers. When that didn't work he pinched him; pinches became fingernails digging in, and then turned into punches. It didn't take Mick long to realize that Rio was seriously pissed. He released his hold on the hose and instead grabbed Rio's wrists and forced him flat to the ground.

Rio kicked and fought. "Let go! Let go, you fucking bastard!"

"Rio, stop it," Mick ordered, shocked at how incensed the young man was. Anger and despair were rolling off Rio in huge waves that beat against Mick's senses. He blanketed Rio with his own body, trying to stop his wild struggles. "You're going to get hurt."

"I don't care. I don't fucking care. Hit me. Go ahead and hit me!"

"I'm not going to hit you!"

"Then get off me! Just fucking leave me alone!"

Releasing his hold, Mick sat up and watched Rio roll away and scramble to his feet. Without another word or a backward glance, Rio walked to the house and disappeared inside. Mick got to his feet, turned off the water, then plopped back down on the damp ground. Viciously cursing under his breath, he was still sitting there when Jed's red truck came up the driveway. He heard his brother get out, but Mick didn't bother looking up when a pair of well-worn athletic shoes and blue jean-clad legs came into his field of vision.

"Well, this is pretty pathetic looking. What the hell are you up to, bro?"

"Not a goddamned thing," Mick growled.

Jed squatted down in front of him. "Why don't you just admit it? This is a big fucking mistake."

"Don't start with me, Jed. We've been through this. I can't touch that kid. It's not the right thing to do no matter what either of us wants."

"You're so damned stubborn. I take it Rio didn't care for your proposal."

"No, he didn't. We got in a fight."

"Well, good for him, but I can see he didn't manage to knock any sense into you."

Mick slid a hand through his wet hair and pushed it back off his forehead. He felt like shit. "Jed, just...cut me some slack. Okay?"

Jed sighed. "All right." He stood and held out his hand. "Come on. Get cleaned up. It'll be a done deal in a few hours. I just hope you can forgive yourself and me when it's over."

Ruthlessly tamping down the emotions that threatened to overwhelm him, Mick grabbed his brother's hand and allowed himself to be hauled to his feet. He led the way to the house and discovered that Rio had dumped his wet clothes in the kitchen sink.

"You two have a water fight?" Jed asked, eyeing Rio's discarded clothes.

"Among other things," Mick replied. He began to strip while Jed wandered into the living room and turned on the television.

Throwing his wet things in the sink on top of Rio's, Mick passed by the small bathroom and heard the shower running. Showering was exactly what he intended to do and, after having withstood the cold water outside, a cold shower inside was nothing to fear.

Afterward dressing in clean clothes, he returned to the living room. Rio was sharing the sofa with Jed and watching television. Grabbing on to his hard-won calm, Mick left them to it and went on to take care of their wet clothes. By this time, the sun was setting and twilight had begun easing the transition from day to night. Carrying their clothes into the small laundry room off the kitchen, he loaded the washer and for a moment immersed himself in the tingling sensation that was moving under his skin.

Absently rubbing a hand over his forearm, he unconsciously sought to ease the sensations that were mildly irritating, yet strangely seductive too. He could feel his own restlessness rising, not to mention the ache that was again building below his belly. The constant and growing need was inescapable. As a mature werewolf he could ignore the arousal and the need to shift. but he rarely did unless it was absolutely necessary. He saw no reason to deny something so pleasant. The transformation not only eased his discomfort but gave him great pleasure. He loved giving the wolf free rein and usually looked forward to these times with anticipation. Tonight was not going to be one of those nights.

Returning to the living room, he found Rio right where he'd left him, but the kid was far from relaxed. From his position in the kitchen, Mick watched as Rio began to unravel. He was sitting on the sofa with both feet planted on the floor and one leg had taken on an almost frantic bounce. Other nervous gestures had begun as well. Rio kept hugging himself, his hands sliding up and down his upper arms as though he was cold. When he seemed to realize what he was doing, he stopped, only to seconds later start an unconscious rocking motion. He was beginning to look like a drug addict going through withdrawal.

Mick looked out the window. Daylight was nearly gone. It wouldn't be long now. His gaze was drawn back when Jed spoke.

"Rio, come here."

Mick immediately took a step forward, his wolf growling in protest. Forcing himself to hang on to his composure, he walked into the living room and sat in a comfortable wing chair across from the sofa. Rio glanced in his direction then rose from the sofa. Jed was sitting back with his thighs spread. He motioned for Rio to take a seat between them. When Rio sat and settled back against Jed, Mick dug his fingers into the arms of the chair.

"That's it. Just relax," Jed softly encouraged.

His hands came up to massage Rio's shoulders and after a few minutes he leaned in and began to nuzzle the back of Rio's neck. Caught between outrage and arousal, Mick sat watching his brother seduce the one person he wanted to claim for himself. His cock filled and throbbed within the tight confines of his jeans, and he wanted to adjust it but couldn't bring himself to move. He was afraid to move. His wolf was so enraged, Mick was almost sure if he released his grip on the chair arms he'd launch himself at his brother. Instead he sat frozen and watched.

Jed took one of his hands from Rio's shoulder and slid it around his torso. Working at the button on Rio's jeans, he freed it then lowered the zipper. He tugged Rio's T-shirt free from the waistband of his jeans and pushed his hand under, sliding it upward. With the rising fabric Mick could see the creamy sheen of Rio's skin and how it contrasted with the tan of Jed's hand. That hand arrived at one of Rio's nipples and Mick could clearly see the fingertips brushing over the tender nub.

His gaze flew to Rio's face and their eyes met. Rio's expression was blank, but his eyes were glittering with unshed tears. Seeing Rio's reaction was like taking a punch in the gut. "Stop. Stop it, Jed," Mick ordered, barely able to keep his voice steady.

"It's about fucking time," Jed told him and immediately ceased. He gently urged Rio away from him and rose from the sofa. "Sorry, Rio. And you," he said, addressing Mick. "Stop being an ass. Apologize to Rio, and you owe me fucking big-time for this."

"I know, I know. Get the fuck out. Right now I've got the urge to hurt you real bad."

"And whose fault is that?"

"Mine, all right? *Jed*. Just go."

"I'm gone. Take it easy on each other, would you?"

In the silence that followed, Mick heard Jed get into his truck, start the engine, and drive off. Only when the sound of the truck died away was he able to take a deep breath. He looked at Rio, but he was looking down at the floor and not meeting Mick's gaze.

"I'm sorry," he began. "That was completely wrong. I never should have asked you to accept something so...so..."

"Stupid?" Rio asked.

"Stupid," Mick agreed.

"I accept your apology, and I'm sorry about earlier. For hitting you."

"I deserved it."

"Yeah, you did." Still not meeting Mick's eyes, Rio rose from the sofa and straightened his clothes.

Instead of sitting back down, he began to wander from place to place, and Mick could tell the coming change was again overriding every other consideration.

"Rio," Mick called, getting his attention. "Come outside and walk with me."

Jerkily nodding his agreement, Rio followed Mick outside. They did a circuit of the outer perimeter of the entire property then began walking among the trees.

"Does it help to move?" Mick asked, breaking the silence between them.

"Yeah, but I still feel like something's crawling under my skin."

"That's normal. After your first change it won't be so bad. It can even be a pleasant sensation."

"Right now it's driving me nuts."

"I know. I remember how it was."

"When did you become a werewolf?" Rio asked.

"I've always been one. I'm a born were."

"So you had to go through this when you were a little kid?"

"Not until puberty hit. That's what triggers the first shift in a born were."

"You're lucky. At least you didn't have to get torn up to become one."

"You shouldn't have had to go through that either. All it takes is a bite, which involves some pain, but it doesn't have to be a traumatic experience. Sutter was insane, Rio. What he did to you was brutal and absolutely abhorred by all self-respecting weres. We don't make it a policy to turn humans against their will. In fact, it's just the opposite."

"I know. I actually read that somewhere, though the article really didn't say why. Guess it was just my luck to meet up with a whackjob werewolf. Uhn!" Rio came to an abrupt halt and clutched at his middle. "Oh damn."

"It's starting," Mick said softly. He looked into the sky. It was full dark and just at the horizon the moon was starting to rise. Fascinated, he watched more of that silver orb appear by infinitely tiny increments. Shaking his head to clear it, he turned back to Rio.

"Your eyes are glowing," Rio breathed.

It suddenly struck Mick why Rio's eyes fascinated him so much. Silver-gray with that hint of deep blue at the rims, they resembled twin moons in the night sky. "Yours will too. Soon," Mick told him. He looked around and nodded with satisfaction. They were standing beside a dense grouping of redbud and wild dogwood trees that formed a crescent shape. Motioning Rio to follow, Mick led them to the inner curve, which faced the back of his property and the farm land beyond. Tree branches fanned over them, enclosing them in a leafy hollow. "This is a good place. Strip." Without waiting for an answer, Mick pulled his T-shirt up and off. He paused with hands at the button of his jeans when he noticed Rio staring at him. "What?"

Rio blinked and shook his head. "Nothing."

Hiding his knowing smile, Mick finished with his undressing first. The look on Rio's face as he openly admired Mick's body had been flattering. Never one to struggle with his body image, it was still good to know his partner was pleased with what he saw when the clothes came off.

Mick seated himself cross-legged on the cool grass, his thoughts shifting along the same lines as Rio's. The silent words he used to caution himself about getting too involved became fainter and fainter as more of Rio's body came into view. To say he liked what he was seeing was an understatement.

Light from the rising moon caressed Rio's parchment-pale skin and created shadows that defined the muscles delineating his torso, arms, and legs. Like Mick's own, Rio's cock was fully erect and bobbed with every move he made. By the time he was completely naked, Mick knew he'd been right when he'd first considered taking this route in getting Rio through the change. This was definitely going to come back to bite him on the ass, but at the moment he didn't give a damn.

When the last of Rio's clothes were discarded, Mick began softly speaking. "Sit in front of me just like this with your knees touching mine."

Rio silently obeyed and hissed when his bottom connected with the ground. "Damn, that's cold."

He wiggled in the grass and Mick smiled. "You'll get used to it. In a moment you'll even like it. Now, relax as much as you can and close your eyes." When Rio did so, Mick continued. "You should begin to feel it now, warmth moving up into your body from the ground. Can you feel it?"

"Yes. What is that?"

"That's the warmth of the Earth embracing you. You've become a very special being, Rio. Weres are nourished by the core energy of this world." Mick brushed his fingers over the cool grass and felt tiny surges of power infuse his skin. "With the changing of your DNA, a pathway opens between your body and the land. The strength you receive, the healing power, all the gifts you've been given are linked with the Earth. You're not only human now, you're animal as well, and animals understand and exist in this world in a way humans could never hope to. Through use of its senses, an animal feels the very heartbeat of the world. It's a rare human who can experience such a thing; most of them are deaf, dumb, and blind to this vital, living entity to which they owe their existence."

He trained his gaze on the young and earnest face before him. Holding so still with his eyes closed, Rio's face reminded Mick of a peaceful visage carved in marble. Suppressing his desire to brush his fingers over the curve of Rio's cheek -- if only to confirm that he was indeed a living, breathing being -- Mick continued, "Listen to me carefully now. The things I'm about to say, I know they may sound archaic and melodramatic to you, but it's tradition. This is the way I was brought through the change. These are the words I was given. It's been this way for generations and this is the way it will continue. Understand?"

"Yes."

"Good. Those shivers of power you feel crawling under your skin is this world holding on to you. The pain you'll suffer is the moon trying to steal you away. She's like a jealous lover, our moon. She sees what her sister Earth has and desires it for herself and so she entices and whispers to you to see her beauty and kneel before her in supplication." As he spoke the words, Mick was drawn back in time to his own first shift. He remembered the images those words invoked and how awed it made him feel to be coveted by two such alluring powers. His heart beat faster at the intensity of that adolescent memory.

"At this time, during the first change when you have no experience to fight it, your body becomes a battleground between the Earth and the moon. A part of you is clinging to the warm and secure familiarity on which you rest, while another part is being seduced by the erotic temptation of she who rises above. After you shift for the first time you'll able to easily balance the influences, but for now, you're about to become a pawn in an ages-old war and you can't let the moon win. If you do, it will drive you mad because you can never reach her, never be one with her. That's why we don't actively strive to turn humans. It's too dangerous. Moon madness is wicked and incurable. The only way to give the sufferer peace is to terminate their life force."

As he spoke, Mick carefully watched Rio who, while attentive to his words, was beginning to again visibly react on a physical level. Once more his body was rocking and his breathing had ratcheted higher. Mick could actually hear the hard thumping of Rio's heart. Rio groaned and his fists clenched. Sweat broke out on his skin and he shivered.

His eyes flew open and Mick calmly met Rio's pained panic. "It hurts. It's really starting to hurt. Bad. It feels like fire burning under my skin."

"I know," Mick soothed. "Come here. Straighten your legs and put them over my thighs." Mick did the same, straightening his legs and sliding them beneath Rio's. They edged closer to each other until their cocks were separated by only inches. Mick reached for Rio's hand and brought it to his own cock, encouraging Rio to hold him. He then wound the fingers of his free hand around Rio's straining erection. "Touch me. Just like this," he growled, and began stroking the firm column of flesh in his hand. Rio's moans struck a spark in Mick's belly and his touch ignited the flame. Rio followed his instruction and they slowly jacked each other.

"You *will* hold tightly to your place in this world, Rio. You're strong, and you owe the Earth your allegiance and your life. Only when you shift will you be allowed to look to the moon. As the wolf you'll lift your head and sing to her, praise her beauty, and offer your regrets for not succumbing to her will," Mick panted, gritting his teeth against the surge of pleasure Rio's touch caused, "but you will not offer more. Do you hear me?"

"Yesss," Rio hissed then groaned. "Oh fuck. Mick!"

Mick's free hand was sliding over the taut muscles of Rio's thigh while Rio's free hand gripped Mick's shoulder. Rio's nearness, his strained moans along with the scent of need and fear rolling off him were driving Mick over the boundary he sought to keep between them. If he leaned forward just a bit, Mick knew he could taste those tempting lips, but he held back, trying desperately to hold on to his earlier resolve. Neither of them needed a lover. Right? That wasn't what this was about.

Even as he continued to try convincing himself of that, his wolf fought him. Wordlessly it projected "*mate, ours, take*" while images of fucking Rio blasted through his mind. His wolf was snarling, snapping at him and tearing at his restraint. Mick became so embroiled in the struggle with his other self, it came as no small surprise when Rio's moans escalated and morphed into a strident cry as he climaxed. The warmth of Rio's seed spilled over Mick's hand and spattered his cock and belly. That wet heat touching him wrenched a low, guttural groan from his throat.

"I'm sorry," Rio gasped, his voice harsh and shaking.

"No reason to be sorry," Mick roughly assured him. "You'll come again."

"No, unhhh," Rio groaned. Mick could feel the ripple that ran through Rio's body as he shook with pain and pleasure. "No. Sorry for this. Sorry you have to do this. Have to touch me."

Confused and hit with a rush of furious denial triggered by something in Rio's tone, Mick gripped the young man's shoulders. "What are you saying?"

"I know," Rio sobbed. "I know I'm no better than a whore. I did things. I did all those bad things. I let myself be used for money. You shouldn't have to touch me."

Horrified, Mick released his grip on Rio's shoulders, slid his hands under his hips and, with an easy lift, brought the pup up and onto his lap. He bent his knees to sit cross-legged again and settled Rio into the hollow cradle that was created by doing so. Gritting his teeth against the pleasure of his young charge's body pressed against his still fully erect cock, Mick concentrated on ripping Rio's self-castigation to shreds. "Don't you ever say that again," he harshly growled. "Don't you know how precious you are? I've had to fight myself not to touch you and not just because you're so beautiful you make me ache, but because you're you…just you. I've held back because I can't let myself hurt you, not when I know everything you've been through. Understand? I don't want you to hurt anymore. Not because of me and my selfish desires."

"But you don't hurt me!" Rio wailed, tears trickling down his cheeks. "When you talk to me, when you touch me, it goes away. All the bad things go away and I feel clean again. Please, don't pull away, don't give me away again."

"Oh, Christ, kid," Pain and elation both curled in the pit of Mick's stomach and tears stung his eyes at Rio's sobbing declaration. He struggled to breathe past the growing lump in his throat until he was distracted once again.

"R-Rio."

"What?" Mick asked, his brow furrowing in confusion.

"N-not kid," Rio sniffed. "I'm…I'm not a kid."

With those words, Mick found himself smiling with the surge of foolish joy that flowed through him. "No. You're not a kid."

Released from his self-imposed chains of restraint, Mick did what he'd been longing to do for days. He cupped Rio's cheeks, wiped the tears from them and brought their lips together. His tongue slid into Rio's welcoming mouth and once more that distinct and decadent flavor went straight to his head. His arms encircled Rio's body and pulled him closer. Rio's flagging erection abruptly stiffened, and they rocked against each other, groaning with each push that brought needed pressure to the rigid length of his cock. Mick breathed in Rio's arousal, the heady musk filling his nostrils and fueling his lust more surely than the moon's siren song.

The kiss ended abruptly with the return of Rio's pain. "Mick! Oh God," Rio cried out, his body going rigid in Mick's arms.

"Hold on to me, baby, hold on. I'm gonna make it better. So much better," Mick promised. Using one hand, Mick slid it down to cup Rio's buttock, then slid farther inward to his crease and let his fingers brush over the tightly clenched entrance between Rio's taut cheeks. "Does it feel good when I touch here?"

Rio whimpered and nodded. "More."

"Are you sure, Rio? I want to fuck you, but if you don't want that…"

"I want you to…but won't it hurt? No lube."

"Don't need it," Mick assured him. "Remember your changing DNA? Your body is undergoing some other, more subtle modifications. Your body secretes a natural lube when you become aroused." Mick eased the tip of one finger into Rio's asshole and pumped it in and out several times. Slippery fluid coated the tight walls that gripped him and he slid his finger in to the root. Rio gasped, then wiggled, obviously trying to take it deeper. "Mmm, see, you're already wet for me. Another perk to becoming a werewolf."

"So gooood," Rio groaned. "Please, more."

"All you can take, pup. Anything for you," Mick whispered against Rio's ear.

With the finger buried inside his hot depths, Mick began to prepare Rio. He pushed his finger forward and back, stroking past the tight outer ring that gripped and over the satiny-smooth inner walls. Eventually, on an outward stroke, he brought two fingers together and sent them both burrowing forward.

Rio groaned and shimmied his hips side to side. "Push it deeper."

"You're awfully demanding," Mick teased, nipping his earlobe.

"Need it. Need you. Come on, Mick. Please? Now?"

Every phrase Rio uttered was punctuated by kisses, licks, and nibbles that were peppered over Mick's cheeks, chin, neck, and shoulders. He tilted his head and sucked in a gasp when Rio's teeth pinched a fold of skin at his throat. The sting of blood being drawn to the surface made his cock throb even harder and he sent a third finger forward to stretch Rio's tight hole.

Rio ground down onto those long, fluted fingers then began a rapid bouncing movement. "If I give you another hickey will you fuck me?" he panted.

"Try it and see," Mick challenged in a gravelly drawl.

Slowing his movements, Rio chose a place on the other side of Mick's throat, set his teeth to the unmarked skin, and set about inciting his lust. That stinging bite got Mick's bold partner just what he asked for. His fingers slithered free and with an easy one-armed boost, Rio was lifted while Mick guided his cock in place. The plump, leaking head nudged Rio's sensitized hole, stretched the taut ring and eased forward until the head lodged inside. Rio's flesh closed firmly around it.

With an ass cheek cupped in either hand, Mick slowly lowered Rio until the liquid heat of his sheath fully engulfed Mick's cock. The feel of that silky-hot flesh wrapping tightly around him was mind-numbingly exquisite. Rio was crying out, arching his back and thrusting his hips against Mick, making those round cheeks flex in Mick's palms with an unconscious sensuality that had him gritting his teeth to keep from coming.

"Easy, baby, easy. Slow down," Mick crooned, wanting to calm their headlong rush to orgasm.

"No! Feels so good. So big. Need to come. Need to come now!" Rio wailed.

Growling to communicate his dominance, Mick wrapped an arm around Rio and firmly settled him in place. His free hand encircled the base of Rio's cock and squeezed. "No more coming until I say so. Obey, pup," Mick ordered.

Whimpering, Rio subsided and sagged against Mick. "But it makes the pain go away."

"I know. That's why we want to make it last. In spite of the fact that you feel like you could come a dozen times, your imagination is outrunning reality. We have to pace ourselves, or by the time you're drawn into the change our capacity for pleasure will be drained and all you'll have left is the pain." Mick released his grip on Rio's cock.

Rio shuddered and groaned. "Are you sure I can't come a dozen times? How about eight or nine?"

"If you can shoot five times within the next two hours it'll be a miracle. Make it four and I'll be impressed. I'll settle for three."

"Two hours? Is that how long it's going to take?"

"I don't really know. It depends on your resistance, which is exactly why I don't want you to think about it anymore. All you're going to think about is how good it feels that I'm touching you." Mick did a shift of his hips that slid his buried cock across the spongy knot of nerves within Rio's passage. That unexpected move had Rio gasping and writhing in his arms. "So how good did that feel?"

The wild surge of pleasure that spilled over Rio's senses blanketed the pain, merged with, and subdued it. He wriggled in Mick's arms, his body undulating in a way that brushed and flexed flesh against flesh, muscle against muscle. The involuntary, bliss-driven motion ground his hips down, burying the thick cock that filled him even deeper. Being taken by Mick made him feel connected on a level far beyond what he'd ever experienced with anyone else.

"Unhhh. Good. So good," he managed to answer, lowering his head to the big man's shoulder.

This joining with Mick encompassed more than just the need for physical release. There was warmth and caring so deep it went beyond the stark sexual encounters he'd had in the past that were nothing but one person's lust being played out upon another. This true intimacy, this loving act, could never be mistaken for such a violation. Rio closed his eyes and held on to Mick while his body absorbed the touches, ate the pleasure and used it to counter the pain. Involuntary tears rolled down his cheeks.

"Don't cry, baby. Is it bad? You want to come again? Hmm?"

"Crying? Who's crying?" Rio gasped when Mick's fingertips played over the head of his cock.

"That would be you. I feel tears against my skin like the night we first met, and I can smell the salt."

Embarrassed, Rio wiped his eyes and sat up straight. "I'm not crying. It's just sweat."

"If you say so, pup. Come here." Mick pulled Rio close, his mouth closing over Rio's right nipple.

"*Oh God.* What are you doing?"

Releasing him for a moment, Mick looked up into Rio's eyes and smiled. "Exactly what it looks and feels like. I've sucked your nipples before."

"I remember, but I'm not a girl, you know."

"I think I figured that out." Mick gave Rio's cock a squeeze that made him squirm. "Now hush and love it like you're supposed to."

That near grouchy growl of an order had Rio on the verge of laughing until Mick's mouth turned it into a moan to go with the pleasure that radiated from the hard little nub on his chest. Rio tilted his head back, his eyes closed as he rocked against Mick. Sensation was flashing through his body like wildfire. He felt hot and heavy, as though the Earth's gravitation was suddenly ruthlessly clutching him. Even immersed as he was in Mick's touch and the heat and need that surrounded him, another presence called. He could feel a cool, insistent phantom demanding his attention. Eyes opening, through the leafy canopy overhead, the glowing orb of the moon filled his vision and with just a glimpse, he was enthralled.

He swayed with the sudden weightless sensation that hit him. Metaphysical bubbles burst beneath his skin. Rio could feel his flesh stretching and contracting as his bones began to shift, but there was nothing else, no fear, no pain, no pleasure, only the need to fly, only the need to be absorbed by the glow from above. It filled his eyes, burrowed into his brain and blinded him. He had to go, had to reach her. He struggled to stand, to push up and away, but something held him, and he snarled as rage instantly flooded him.

Strong arms kept him prisoner and Rio fought even as a voice hurled itself like a rock against the glassy surface of the silvery orb of light that encompassed his very being. That powerful voice hammered cracks in the budding madness that sought to hold him and Rio cried out when his glowing prison shattered. Pain crashed over him in a violent storm, turning his cry into a scream.

"Damn you! You're not going anywhere! Do you hear me? Feel this. Feel this, Rio!"

Mick's voice sliced through the pain. His touch ripped the fabric of agony that covered Rio and drenched it with a pleasure that soaked the encompassing weave and picked apart the threads of exquisite torture being visited upon him. Jolted by the panicked fury of Mick's outrage, Rio ceased struggling against him. Fingers wrapped around his cock and began stroking. Rio arched into that almost too vigorous grasp, crying out at the rapid rise of near orgasmic waves of pleasure that smashed and hurtled over every barrier in the way to become the full-fledged climax that roared over him.

All his thoughts and fears were swept away by that broiling wave. What remained was his body, a mass of quivering muscles, flesh and shifting bones. His hot, sweaty skin began to sprout fur and his senses expanded almost painfully, sight, smell, taste. The scent of male rut and freshly expelled semen compelled his erection to stay iron hard while his inner passage clenched and rippled around the hard bar of Mick's cock as though prepared to strangle it in an effort to keep it buried deep within him. Exquisite swells of sensation born of pleasure and pain yanked whimpering moans from the depths of his chest while his body shuddered again and again.

Rio's world, already a whirling maelstrom from the effect of his coming and the impending shift, tilted as, with an effortless heave, Mick repositioned them. Rio cried out when the overheated skin of his back hit the cool grass but it wasn't left there long enough to absorb the earth's warmth. Instead he was rolled to his stomach, where insistent hands pulled at his hips and drew him up on his knees.

One of those hands shifted position and found his cock while the other was positioned at the nape of his neck. Before his befuddled mind could form a thought, Mick's cock again slid deep inside from behind while his body blanketed Rio from thighs to shoulders. Another wild wave of orgasmic sensation shot through him at Mick's penetration, and Rio squirmed and wriggled to take more of the hard column of throbbing flesh that filled him.

"Close your eyes," Mick growled. "Don't you dare even try to look up. Breathe in, Rio. Smell the grass, the trees and the earth. Take in the air. Can you smell it? Taste it? There's a rabbit nearby and deer. Can you smell them? When you change, we'll hunt."

Rio could smell everything Mick pointed out and more. His head spun with the amount of new stimuli his overtaxed brain was trying to process. The world was spreading itself out before him like a buffet to be sampled and savored, but the multitude of choices forced upon him left him feeling like a glutton on the verge of being ill.

"Did you hear that?" Mick insisted as he forced Rio to accept his place. "An owl. It's miles away but you can hear it, can't you? And the water? There's a stream that runs through a stand of trees about a quarter of a mile away. The water's cold and clear. I'll take you there and we'll drink. This is your world, this is where you belong and, by God, you're not going anywhere."

Mick's hips had begun a merciless pumping that shoved his thick cock deep within Rio's passage until he withdrew, only to bury himself again and again. The hand that gripped Rio's cock endlessly stroked, demanding his reaction, his participation, his pleasure, and his seed.

Rio bucked and writhed beneath the blissful, aching punishment being visited upon him. Mick's words penetrated as surely as his cock and though he understood, Rio found himself unable to respond. His mouth felt strange, his tongue and teeth alien. Through eyes that peered through barely opened lids, he saw his fingers contract as fur emerged from every pore to cover them and sharp claws sprouted from the nubs that had once been human digits.

His entire body was enveloped in an alien shift and slide as it melted and reformed. Through it all, burning pain raked across every nerve ending even as another orgasm gathered momentum in his gut and burst free. Rio's wailing cry became a stuttering howl. He felt the hot wash of Mick's semen spray his clutching passage and heard his harsh groan of release. Rio's seed pumped forth in spurts to drench the grass beneath him and with a last wrenching jet, he collapsed to the ground.

Mouth open, he lay panting, his body quivering from head to toe as the final ripples of his first shift faded away amid the echoes of pleasure and pain. When his mind began to clear, his first thought was to wonder how a blanket came to be between him and cool grass. Not that he minded. He'd had enough of that gut-wrenching shock when cold grass and hot skin made contact. Still, his curiosity was aroused and so he wearily lifted his head. A quick glance down the length of his body left him stunned and breathless. He was no longer human. The self he was so familiar with was gone and had been replaced by something distinctly canine. Wolf.

Blind panic overwhelmed him, and he began to thrash around in an effort to stand. Some instinct, awakened and driven by fear, screamed at him to run, but his limbs wouldn't cooperate. They felt clumsy and uncoordinated, while his body felt heavy as lead. Involuntary whines poured from his open mouth as he struggled and fought until a hand landed on his shoulder and a well-remembered voice spoke to him.

"Easy now. Stop that. Just rest a moment, Rio. You need to just rest a minute and let the rest of the shift work through you."

Hearing that voice, feeling that touch, sent Rio's panic fleeing. His straining muscles and turmoil-driven mind gave in to that calming admonition. Mick was still here. Mick would know what to do; he'd make it right. Of that, Rio had no doubt and so he subsided and lay quiescent, letting exhaustion have its way with him. Lying still and silent proved to be a very good thing. Mick continued to pet him and the touch of his hand was calm and soothing.

"I had a feeling you'd make a beautiful wolf. I was right," Mick softly commented and Rio actually felt his ears perk up. The unfamiliar movement sent a trickle of amusement through him. If it were possible he would have laughed; instead, he lay quietly while the unexpected and giddy sensations flowed over him. "Most of your fur is like cream tipped with silver. We'll have to be careful no one sees you. They'll be wanting to make a coat out of you."

A growl rose up in Rio's throat and when he voiced it, Mick laughed. "Don't worry. We won't let that happen. You should be able to get up now. I'm going to shift and we'll take some time to get you acquainted with your new form."

Cautiously Rio moved and found that Mick was right; his body no longer felt as though it was anchored to the ground, and his limbs moved at his direction. He got to his feet, all four of them, and took a few unsteady steps. As he moved, another presence loomed larger in his mind. The being that went with this body, his other self, awoke and took control. Rio felt his human half submerge, but it wasn't an unpleasant sensation, rather a kind of pleasant dream state in which he was still fully aware but without the responsibility of making the decisions to move or to act. It was strangely relaxing and he sank into this new role like an overworked laborer into an easy chair at day's end.

His wolf's awareness flared up and out in a burst of joy that had Rio voicing a silent laugh while his new body began cavorting and dancing. Both minds merged and lost themselves to the pure ecstasy of being until a rumbling growl brought them up short. Rio fell to earth with a metaphorical thump while his wolf tensed and turned. Both entities froze together in awe.

The wolf that stood before him was magnificent. Large and powerful, even beneath the thick coat of fur, his heavy musculature was evident. His coloring ranged from shades of cream to black and russet. The paler fur around his eyes accented the bluish green tint of eyes that gazed at Rio with an expectant intensity. When Rio did nothing, the wolf's muzzle wrinkled, his mouth parting to reveal pearly white teeth and razor-sharp canines while a displeased, warning growl rumbled up from the depths of his barrel-like chest.

While the human half began to panic, the wolf half knew just what to do. Even as the knowledge formed in his mind, the young wolf that Rio had become dropped down and crawled to his alpha where he groveled and rolled, presenting his throat and belly. The older wolf deigned to lower his head, allowing the young one to lick his face. He opened his mouth and closed his jaws firmly over the young one's muzzle, shook him lightly then released him and stood back. Secure now in his alpha's approval, the youngster leaped to his feet and danced around. With the formalities taken care of, his alpha turned and loped away and the young wolf followed without hesitation.

For the next few hours Rio watched in a dreamy daze as he was carried along on a journey few humans ever got to take. As a wolf, he ran across fields and among trees. His senses were so finely tuned he could detect the scents of animals, plants, water, and anything else that came within range. He could tell if what he smelled was near or far and, in the case of animals, if they had been there recently or even hours or days since. Even though it was night, his vision allowed him to move freely through the trees and brush without fear of tripping over anything.

When a rabbit broke cover, the alpha gave chase. Startled, the young wolf hesitated then chased after them, catching up in time to see his leader dispatch the rabbit with a shake and a single crunch from powerful jaws. The body was torn open and meat and blood consumed. Curious and suddenly hungry, the new wolf crept forward, low to the ground, whining for permission. After a few growls, the alpha male gave way and the younger wolf pounced.

The taste of blood and raw meat was confusing. Part of him loved it, while the other struggled not to retch. Rio compromised by submerging himself as deeply as possible while clearing his human mind, giving free rein to his other self. It worked and when the rabbit was consumed, as promised by Mick, his alpha led him to a stream and they drank fresh clear water that tumbled over mossy stones. In the shallows at the edge where the water remained calm and placid, the young wolf saw the reflection of a glowing orb.

Lifting his head, the moon swam into view and a wave of ineffable sadness and gratitude swept over him. His sat back on his haunches and gave voice to the emotions that swamped him. He instinctively understood that the moon drew forth his change and therefore, in a way, served as midwife to the birth of this part of himself. Though he could never truly give himself to her, he could pay this small tribute and did. The haunting, mournful tune he sang became a chorus as the alpha joined in. In the distance, dogs and a pack of coyotes too echoed the wolves' sentiments.

Surprised and pleased, the young wolf let his song die away and listened with a doglike grin to the distant howls. It seemed appropriate somehow. When the cries died away and the alpha nudged him, he followed without demur.

By the time they returned to the place their journey had begun, the young wolf was exhausted. He flung himself down in the sheltered space among the trees where he'd begun his life and curled in upon himself with his tail draped over his nose. Contentment filled him when his alpha lay beside him and he slept with the scent of the big male filling his nostrils.

* * *

Rio woke slowly and stretched. The mattress beneath him was firm, the sheet draped over him was soft, and the body pressed along the length of his back and thighs was solid and warm. His head rested against one of Mick's arms while the other arm was draped over Rio's waist, the fingers of his hand splayed loosely over Rio's stomach. With a sleepy murmur, he snuggled deeper and pressed back into the man holding him. Mick's scent was warm and musky, arousing yet comforting, and every part of Rio stayed relaxed but one. His cock stirred and thickened, growing hard and demanding. Wanting to ignore it in favor of going back to sleep, Rio couldn't discount the other cock that was filling against his backside. It seemed he wasn't the only one waking up.

"Mmm, morning." Mick nuzzled the back of his neck and the warm rumble of his words stirred the short hairs at Rio's nape.

A small shiver caused Rio's shoulders to do a tiny shimmy and he smiled when Mick chuckled against his skin. "Morning. Though I don't want get up."

Mick's hand slid down a few inches to find Rio's obvious erection. "Feels like you're already up."

"Umm, that part, yeah." Rio moved his hips to the lazy rhythm of Mick's caressing hand, closing his eyes to appreciate the swirls of pleasure that danced beneath his belly. He noted the raspy roughness of his own voice and wondered if it was from the various vocalizations from the night before. Not that it bothered him in the least. There was a lot to be said for howling at the moon and moaning like a porn star while having the best sex of your life. Even if that sex had been marred by pain, it was a pain based in necessity and not malicious intent, which made all the difference. "How did we end up here?" he asked a bit breathlessly. What Mick was doing felt wonderful, but it wasn't enough to steal his senses. Yet.

"I carried you in. You reverted to human about an hour after you fell asleep. You hardly stirred or made a peep when I picked you up and put you to bed."

"It was a strenuous night."

"For you, yes. How do you feel now? Anything sore?"

Rio moved a bit more vigorously and flexed various muscles without a twinge. "Nope."

"What about here?" Mick released Rio's cock and slid his hand over the young man's hip. Insinuating it between them, he nudged his fingers into the crease of Rio's ass and let his fingertips play over his taut entrance.

"Unnn, no, not sore," Rio breathed, and pushed back trying to capture those elusive fingers.

"Want me inside? Is it all right?"

"Yes, want you."

"What parts of me?"

"All of you."

"What parts of me here," Mick insisted, letting the tip of one finger ease inside Rio's twitching hole.

"Mmm, yesss," Rio breathed, wriggling into Mick's touch. "Fingers, cock."

"Tongue?"

Rio almost swallowed his own tongue at the urgent surge of hot desire that shot through him. "You'd...you'd do that?"

"Remember what I said last night? Anything for you." Mick slid his tongue over the whorls of Rio's ear. He dipped it inside and made several fuck-like motions with it before capturing Rio's earlobe and giving it a nibbling bite. "Roll over on your stomach and get up on your knees."

That deep and sultry-voiced order and the hot breath that teased his ear had Rio ready to start with the moaning again even though they'd just begun. He followed Mick's instructions and turned over, but before he could get his knees under him Mick leaned over him and held him in place.

"Just stay like this for a minute," Mick ordered with a husky drawl.

Rio felt movement as Mick rose over him and straddled his body. The big man rested lightly against him and Rio could tell he was being careful not to relinquish his full weight on top of him. Large, warm hands began massaging his shoulders and back. Rio sighed and relaxed into the pleasure of Mick's touch, letting his mind drift. Warm breath, soft lips, and a teasing tongue began making a slow foray down his spine. Everything was fine, more than fine for a while, until the easy calm within which Rio rested began to change. The touches that had been bringing him such pleasure slowly morphed. Mick's heat and scent faded while his arousing touches became instead, contact that had to be endured.

Fine tension filled Rio's body even as a familiar icy calm engulfed him. He could feel himself shutting down though part of him began to vigorously protest. *No! I want this! Want him!* Rio opened his mouth, needing to voice the desperate denial that was building inside, but nothing would come out. His vocal cords were frozen by the horrified realization of what was happening.

Possibly alerted by Rio's unnatural silence or the fine tremors that shook him, Mick apparently realized that something was wrong. Rio could clearly hear the concern in Mick's voice when he called out, "Rio? Can you hear me? Are you all right?" Mick moved and suddenly Rio found himself turned and lifted. His trembling body was engulfed in Mick's arms as he was settled in what was quickly becoming a blessedly familiar lap. "It's okay. It's okay, baby. Take it easy. Just breathe, Rio. Just breathe."

The invisible ice that had engulfed his very bones melted away and Rio raised shaking arms to wrap around Mick while laying his cheek against Mick's firm, supportive chest. He took a deep, stuttering breath. "Sorry. I'm sorry. I don't know why... this wasn't supposed to happen. Not now. Not with you. *I don't understand!*" His last sentence was rife with the helpless anxiety he could feel rising to choke him.

"Hey, take it easy. Let's not panic. I'm not exactly sure what's going on, so why don't you take a few more deep breaths and explain it to me, okay?"

Despising the need to do so, Rio forced himself to tell Mick about things he'd rather not remember, much less discuss. "When I...when I was hustling, I hated it. I didn't want to be there so I did this thing, I shut myself off. I gave them my body but nothing else. I wouldn't let them touch me, *me*, the me inside." He paused for a moment as his throat tried to close with the emotions that stirred inside. Taking a few deep breaths, he pushed on. "But I didn't want it to happen now. Not with you, not after last night. Why would I do that? I can't...I didn't want it to happen, but I couldn't control it." Rio felt his fear and dismay deepening. What if he couldn't turn this off? Was he doomed to never be able to feel anything now that he'd finally found someone he actually wanted to share himself with?

"Well, that's a relief. I thought maybe you were afraid of me now that your wolf wasn't taking the lead," Mick told him, putting a damper on Rio's runaway panic. "I'm glad to know you didn't freeze me out on purpose."

"No! I didn't! I swear I didn't."

"Hey, calm down. I believe you." Mick hugged him tight and rocked their bodies comfortingly. "Let's just think about this for a minute. Let's take one point at a time and calmly examine it. We're two intelligent people. We can manage that, can't we?"

Rio sat up a little straighter and took a deep breath. Mick's matter-of-fact attitude was helping him recover his composure. "Yeah, okay, go."

"All right. Point one. You conditioned yourself to react this way when you're having sex, right?"

"Yes."

"Point two. The reason you did it was because you didn't like your partners and the circumstances under which you were forced to have sex, right?"

"Yes."

"Knowing that, the first question we pose should probably be, do you really want to have sex with me? Even though we did it last night, those were special circumstances. It doesn't mean you *have* to do anything now. It's your choice, you know that, don't you?"

"I know. I want to."

"No doubts?"

"No doubts."

"You say that with such conviction, but are you absolutely sure?" Mick caught Rio's gaze with his own. "You've been through so much. I can't help but think that you'd be more likely to hate sex, no matter who you're with."

Rio shook his head and addressed the worry he could plainly see in Mick's eyes. "I don't hate it, but I did learn from it. Sex can be good or bad; it can make you feel good or it can be painful. It all depends on who you're with and what their intentions are. I know you don't want to hurt me. That's why I'm not afraid with you."

This time it was Mick who shook his head. "You...amaze me. You know that? I'm continually surprised at how you've managed to keep your head on straight."

"Apparently it's not totally straight; otherwise I wouldn't be doing the freeze act with you."

"All things considered, I don't have any room for complaint. I'm glad you found a way to protect yourself and maybe it was that that's kept you so clearheaded. So now we just need to address how to solve the problem."

"And how do we do that?"

"I'd say we go about it in a way that makes you constantly aware of who you're with."

"I don't understand."

"We don't do anything that takes me out of your sight. No doggy-style, that kind of thing. We make sure you remain totally aware of me, even if you close your eyes. Use those newly developed senses. Your sense of smell is so much more sensitive now. That should be especially useful in letting you know that it's me who's touching you."

"I hate this, it's stupid," Rio said, directing his gaze across the room. He really didn't want to look at Mick right now. It was too humiliating.

"You're just embarrassed. It's a lot easier to do something like this rather than sit around talking about it, I know that. But as you get older you realize that guessing games in certain situations lead to nothing but misunderstandings and mistakes. I learned to bite the bullet and be honest. I mean, look what almost happened last night because I forgot all that. I tried to fool myself into believing this connection between us didn't exist. I even went so far as to give you over to my brother rather than admit to myself how much I care about you."

"You care about me? You really do?" Mick's admission induced a sense of shy wonder.

"More than just care. My wolf tried to tell me the first time I met you that you were my mate, but I wouldn't listen. I didn't want to listen. I didn't want to want you."

Rio swallowed the pain that hit him square in the chest, lowered his eyes, and merely nodded his understanding.

"Rio." Mick slid his hand under Rio's chin and brought them face-to-face. Their eyes met. "It wasn't because of you. Never because of you or anything you did. It was me. Losing Maddy hurt so much I…I couldn't face the idea of once again caring about someone so much that I'd feel like dying if something happened to them." He gave Rio a resigned smile. "But you wouldn't have that and my wolf definitely wasn't going to sit still for it. I kept telling myself that you were a lost and abused little pup that needed my protection and all the while I was fighting the urge to carry you off to bed. It was pretty damn obvious that I wasn't going to have my way, but I can be very stubborn at times. You may as well know that now."

"I already figured that out," Rio told him, giving his lover a shy yet ironic smile.

"Yeah, well, the kicker came when I tried to pass you over to Jed. Though it was my own stupid idea, remembering how he touched you makes me want to beat the crap out of him even now."

Rio laughed at the wash of pure happiness that swept over him.

"So what do you say? Are you willing to try to make a go of it with me?"

Wrapping his arms around Mick's neck, Rio gave him a pleased peck on the lips. "My wolf votes yes…and so do I."

"Two votes to none. Looks like I win."

Mick took Rio's fleeting kiss and added to it. Their lips came together and their tongues engaged in a slow exploration, each of the other. Even though he was now partly canine, Rio felt like purring and arching when Mick's big hands moved over him, firmly caressing the long, sleek muscles of his back. Reluctantly disengaging from their kiss, he asked, "So what do we do about my problem?"

"I think we should experiment," Mick replied. His teasing smile had Rio suspiciously narrowing his eyes.

"Experiment how?"

"Remember last night when you were sitting in my lap?"

"Yeah."

"Let's try that again with a little variation."

With a few breathless adjustments that had Rio again wanting to moan out loud, he ended up on his knees, straddling Mick's outstretched legs and sitting on his thighs. His arms were draped over Mick's shoulders and Rio couldn't resist resting against his newly acknowledged mate for a moment. It was erotic to have all that naked flesh pressed against his own. Though he knew they'd been in this position before, now that there was no pain, no pending shift to distract him, everything felt so much more clear and intense. He was considerably more aware of Mick and leaned back to peruse the extensive physical attributes of the man who was now his.

While clothed, Mick's body was impressive; naked, he was simply awe-inspiring. His arms, legs, and torso were all finely sculpted muscle and firm, warm flesh. Rio's skin looked pale against the golden hue of Mick's, and that contrast was visually sensual. Where his own chest was smooth, Mick's had a light dusting of dark hair that Rio discovered totally turned him on. There was also a faint trail that ran from below his navel to his pubic bush and what grew from that bush was truly breathtaking. Mick's cock was fully erect, long, thick and solid. The flushed, plum-shaped head showed a bit of crystal fluid welling from the tiny slit and the sight of it actually made Rio's mouth water. There was another part of him too, that was not unaffected and Rio felt the convulsive twitch of the taut and tiny entrance between his butt cheeks. Had that monster prick really been inside him last night? At this point in time it was hard to believe.

Letting his gaze return to meet Mick's, Rio impulsively raised his hands and brought them to Mick's face. With light strokes he traced the contour of his mate's brow, the curve of his cheeks and the solid line of his jaw and chin. It was a face unique in its beauty and maturity and Rio recognized, now more than ever, that his lover was a truly exceptional man. While physical appearance was part of it, it was what shone from his blue-green eyes that truly made Rio realize how lucky he was. There was heat and banked passion, yes, but caring and concern and something else so clearly expressed. He saw something that made it hard to breathe, something that had him on the verge of tears because no one had ever looked at him like this before.

Embarrassed by such an unprecedented and revealing lapse in his defenses, Rio lowered his hands to Mick's shoulders and looked away. "Now what?" he asked.

Mick was right. Having to do things this way, actually thinking about and talking about each move before it was made, had him feeling strangely bashful. It also had him doing things he'd never have thought he'd do. It was good but a little bit disturbing in the bargain as well. Rio felt like he'd made one too many trips on a roller coaster at an amusement park and his head was beginning to spin.

Mick tried to catch Rio's gaze, but Rio steadfastly refused to meet his eyes. "Hey, don't tell me my sassy, smart-mouthed little wolf is turning shy on me."

"Am not. Don't be stupid."

"I'm not, and deny it all you want, you *are* sweet."

"Shit."

The flat, resigned denial expressed in that one word had Mick chuckling. "As for what we do now, a kiss would be nice. You know, I've got a serious fetish going with your lips. They are *so* sexy. So plump and ripe and totally edible."

Surprise had Rio forgetting his reluctance. His gaze flew to Mick's. That oh so serious and intent look in Mick's eyes, in combination with his words, wreaked havoc on Rio's insides. Everything was getting hot, tight and tingly. "Do you have to say stuff like that?" he plaintively asked while his stomach did a few strange flip-flops.

"No, I don't have to, but I want to. You see, I need you to know just how much I want you. I don't want you to slip away from me again. I want you to need to be here with me so badly that you won't be able to even *consider* the possibility of disappearing." Mick slipped a hand behind Rio's head, brought their lips close together and murmured, "Say my name."

The sensuous chill that swept down Rio's spine drastically contrasted with the warm puff of air that caressed his lips. His lips parted and, taking a shallow breath, he said the name. "Mick."

"Do you want me?"

"Yes."

"Say it."

"I want you."

"Say, I want you, Mick."

"I want you, Mick."

"That's right. Don't forget who's holding you. Taste me, Rio. Feel me."

"Bossy," Rio breathed, and closed his eyes.

Mick's husky chuckle vibrated against Rio's mouth as he brought their lips together in one soft, tangible kiss followed by another and another until their parted lips clung and Mick's tongue slipped into Rio's mouth. *Oh God. So good.* There wasn't any question at all that he'd drift away and leave this behind. The flavor that teased his senses and caressed his palate made Rio realize just how hungry he was. It seemed as though he'd been starving for a very long time. The banquet that was set out before him was not only delicious, it wasn't just waiting for him to partake. It was serving itself up to be freely devoured.

He tightened his grip on this sensuous man and met Mick's tongue with his own. The moans he'd suppressed were now generously given without him even being aware of it until he realized those helpless, sensual noises were his own. They only increased when strong hands and sinuous fingers began caressing his body. Those roving hands slid over his shoulders and back. Exploring fingertips took a path down his spine, doing a firm, rolling massage that sent pleasure radiating from the center of his back outward. Mick's hands eventually curled over and cupped the cheeks of his ass, squeezing and rubbing.

His mouth parted from Rio's. "I could almost hold this narrow little ass of yours in one hand," he growled against Rio's ear.

"I'm not that skinny," Rio denied, doing a squiggly little move that ground his butt against Mick's hands.

"You could stand to gain a few pounds, but I admit you feel pretty good just as you are. So how are we doing? You still with me?"

"All the way."

"Mmm, glad to hear it. Say my name again."

"Why? You think I don't remember who you are?" Rio asked with a smile. He loved the way Mick was looking at him. It made his heart beat faster and his chest feel tight, but it was oh so good to be seen. To truly be seen.

"No. I just like how it sounds."

"Oh. Well. How about you give me a reason to say it?"

"You mean like if I do something like this?" Mick released his grip on one of Rio's ass cheeks, brought his hand around, took Rio's hard cock in his hand and gave it a squeeze before starting a series of caressing strokes.

"Oh fuck. *Mick.*"

"Oh yeah. I like the way that sounds."

"If you keep doing that I'm gonna come."

"Really? You gonna give me some cream, baby?"

"Unnn, *stop*, seriously, I'm gonna come," Rio panted, his hips helplessly moving in time with Mick's hand as it slid up and down his cock. Rio could feel his climax coming. Gut-deep tension was winding tighter and tighter and would soon become an explosion of pleasure.

"Do you really want me to stop?"

"Ummm…ahhh…nooo."

"I didn't think so. Just let yourself go. Hold on to me. Hold on tight. We're gonna make a little change."

Rio had barely registered Mick's words when his perception of up and down was taken for a ride. Mick lay back then rolled, bringing Rio under him. The heavy bulk of Mick's weight was lifted away before he had a chance to acknowledge it pressing him down into the mattress. Mick adjusted his position and ended with his head between Rio's thighs. It was all happening so fast Rio didn't even have time to imagine the possibilities of such a position until a hot mouth engulfed his aching cock.

"*Son of a bitch*," he groaned and reached down to grasp at Mick's hair with one hand while the other fisted the sheet beneath him.

Rio closed his eyes and concentrated on the feel of heat and wet generated by Mick's mouth and tongue as it worked up and down his hard length. Mick's downward strokes employed a swirling motion of the tongue while the upward strokes concentrated a long, firm swipe to the underside of Rio's cock. The pressure and suction drew at him with greater and greater urgency, encouraging him to shoot his load.

His hips began moving, thrusting up into the hot encasing sleeve of Mick's tightly pursed lips. Adding his own movements to Mick's merely succeeded in driving his need higher. "Oh God, oh God. Mick. *Mick*!" The hard knot of pleasure that gathered beneath his belly pulsed in a throbbing rhythm then burst in aching spasms. Spurts of semen rushed up and out of his trembling cock with each harsh throb, and Rio arched into the spearing shafts of ecstasy that pierced him.

Panting and gasping for air, his body absorbed the pleasure and shuddered with the penetrating sensations until they diminished. Straining muscles slowly relaxed and feeling as though his bones were dissolving, Rio melted against the mattress.

A hand settled over his, the one he still had fisted in Mick's hair. With a few final licks, Mick released Rio's cock from his mouth and murmured against his damp skin, "Let go, baby, you're gonna rip my hair out, and I'm not sure how long it would take to grow back."

"Sorry, sorry," Rio panted. He struggled to get his elbows under him so he could look down at Mick. "It just felt so good."

"I'm glad you think so. I want you to feel good."

Mick nuzzled his cheek against Rio's inner thigh then kissed a pathway to his balls. Again that talented mouth and tongue went to work, first lapping at the tender skin before pulling first one then the other into his mouth. Rio's balls were lightly sucked and rolled before being released where the cooler air wafted against them, making him quiver, moan, and drop back to the bed.

"I still want to taste you down here." Mick's tongue did a teasing swipe down the strip of flesh that led to Rio's entrance. "Are you all right?"

"I…uh…yeah. Fuck, Mick. I just came."

"So? What's the problem? You're an eighteen-year-old walking hormone. You'll be hard again in thirty seconds."

"Maybe forty-five, but are you sure you wanna…?"

"Oh, I definitely want to. You just lay back and relax, but if you feel like you're going to freeze up on me, grab my hair again or kick me or something."

"All right."

With curiosity and anticipation rising within him, Rio lay back. Mick adjusted his position, rose up on his knees and pushed Rio's lower body upward from the bed. Using his thumbs to part the firm cheeks in his hands, he lowered his head. Rio waited breathlessly then jerked his hips and moaned when Mick's tongue connected with the outer edges of his sensitive hole. The things that wet, sinuous organ could do were amazing. There were long, caressing swipes, short, fleeting laps, and probing strokes that loosened the tight ring of muscle that guarded his needy passage.

Rio could feel himself opening up to accept more and more of the hot tongue that penetrated and explored his quivering entrance. His cock lived up to Mick's prediction that he'd be hard again in thirty seconds. Not only was he hard, but the need building within was driving him crazy. If it wasn't for the fact that Mick had him bent nearly double, he'd be thrashing around in the sheets. As it was, he had them fisted so tightly in his hands he heard and felt the fabric rip.

Astonished, he blinked his eyes open, raised his head and tried to focus on his hands, but the overwhelming arousal had him so distracted he couldn't concentrate. Head dropping back to the pillow, his passion-flooded brain decided it was time to start begging.

"Mick...oh God...Mick, please...mmm...fuck...oh God, it's too good. I can't stand it. Fuck me...please, fuck me...fuck me *now.*"

The response he garnered was a rumbling growl. Mick withdrew his tongue from Rio's quivering hole, swept it over the sleek strip of skin that met the base of his tightening sac and upward over his balls to the base of his cock. The trip didn't end there but continued up the length of his cock where his tongue lingered on the sensitized head before Mick dropped his mouth down, took Rio's cock deep, and swallowed. The compressing massage of Mick's throat worked over Rio's cock and had him crying out while tossing his head on the pillow.

*"Unnn, ahhh, God, Mick! Please, oh fuck, pleeeaaase!!"*

Mick slid his mouth up and off Rio's cock with a parting lick to the flushed and swollen head. He straightened up and lowered Rio's ass to rest on his thighs. "I'm hearing my name quite a bit. Guess you aren't having trouble remembering it's me you're with, huh?"

"No, I'm not," Rio panted, and hoarsely grumbled, "quit fucking around." He looked down the length of his body. His knees were bent and his thighs were parted. Between them he could see Mick's lower body and his vision arrowed to the part he was most interested in at the moment. Mick's cock. It looked huge and hard. The tip was glistening with leaking precum and was flushed a reddish purple. Rio felt so open and so needy that Mick's size was not daunting in the least. "Give me that," he demanded.

"What? This?" Mick asked, fisting his erection.

"Yes, that, goddamn it."

"You get grumpy when you're denied, don't you?"

*"Mick!"*

"Far be it from me to deny you." Mick edged a bit closer and rubbed the head of his cock over Rio's wet entrance. "Did you like my tongue here?"

"You know I did."

"Mmm, I liked the desperation in your voice. We'll definitely be doing that again, but for now…"

Mick lifted one of Rio's legs, spreading him wider and brought it up to rest on his shoulder. His free hand curled around Rio's upper thigh. The other guided his cock, pressing inward only to withdraw then move forward again. Each repetition caused Rio's hole to stretch a bit wider and Mick's cock to slip in a bit deeper until Rio's muscles relaxed and the head was swallowed by his clutching passage. His inner muscles immediately clamped down.

"*Oh fuck*," Rio groaned, breathing in short, sharp pants. "Was it that big before?"

"Same cock," Mick answered. "Damn, you're tight. Just…*oh man*…just try and relax."

Rio could hear the strain in Mick's voice and was glad to know his lover wasn't as unaffected as he pretended to be. Consciously forcing himself to breathe rather than hold his breath, Rio shifted his hips. That small movement caused the thick column of flesh that sought entrance to shift. It slid forward and the pleasurable relief Rio felt caused his grasping passage to relax. With a long, sleek, glide, Mick was fully seated.

"*Oh, yeah,*" Mick groaned. "Feels like I'm melting straight into you."

"M-m-melting? Nooo. Filling...big...hot...*God!*" Unable to stop himself, Rio began rocking his hips, trying his best to ride the thick cock that was buried so deeply within him. His efforts were rewarded when Mick began thrusting in and out. His well-lubricated passage made it easy for Mick's smooth strokes to gain a steady momentum until he achieved and maintained a pounding rhythm. Not wanting this untamed and carnal pleasure to end too soon, Rio struggled to suppress the growing sensations that pulsed below his belly.

As Mick's cock continued to slide deep within him, he kept his gaze on his mate. The expression on his face, intense and sensual, in combination with the passionate fire that shone so fiercely in his eyes, mesmerized Rio. To be the object of such desire made his entire body burn. Eventually it became too much and so he closed his eyes but even that was a mere shallow escape.

Mick's scent, that spicy musk so wild and provocative, invaded Rio's senses with every breath he took. His touch, and not just at that place where their bodies were joined but everywhere, electrified Rio's nerve endings sending countless, infinitesimal pulses of tingling need speeding over his sweat-dampened flesh. Rio felt Mick shift his position a moment before hot breath misted over his parted lips. His lover's mouth took possession, and Mick's tongue invaded to forcefully seduce his own.

When their lips parted, Mick tightly rasped, "Look at me."

Unable to resist that unyielding order, Rio opened his eyes and groaned with the hot rush of pure sexual bliss that shot straight to his gut. "You shouldn't have...I can't stop...I'm gonna come."

"Let me help with that," Mick offered with a husky, breathless drawl.

Long fingers wrapped themselves around Rio's tensely quivering erection. With a few strokes counterpoint to the hard, pounding thrust of Mick's cock within his highly sensitized passage, the balance Rio had barely managed to maintain was overthrown. With a wailing cry, he came. His body arched into the hot rush of sensation that jolted through him even as his cock unleashed spurt after spurt of rich, pearly seed. Wet warmth not only spattered over his torso but drenched his quivering, clasping insides as Mick followed him to completion.

The sound of Mick's guttural groan caused Rio's clenching muscles to tighten even more, yanking free every drop of semen stored within his tightly contracted balls. He shuddered and jerked against his mate, his hoarse cries punctuating the rhythmic expulsion of his hot cream. For a moment there was only heat and sweat and overwhelming pleasure. It ended all too soon but left behind a satisfaction so complete, Rio found himself smiling.

He started to chuckle. Both men groaned when the contractions caused by Rio's amusement forced Mick's waning erection to slide free. Rio quieted, though the smile remained on his face while Mick eased over and dropped down at his side. The two of them lay side by side while their heartbeats calmed and their laboring lungs recovered.

"What was so funny?" Mick finally asked.

"I just feel good," Rio confessed and glanced over when Mick rolled to his side. The smile Mick wore made Rio grin. "What?"

"Nothing, really. I'm just glad you feel good."

"You did it."

"We did it."

Rio nodded. "We did it."

"Wanna do it again?"

Rio laughed, but before he could answer, the phone rang.

# Chapter Five

"So that was your mom?" Rio asked.

From his place on the bed, Mick watched his young mate don a T-shirt. While he talked with his mother, Rio had slipped out of bed and taken a shower. It was rather disappointing. Mick had wanted to share that shower with him, but he couldn't very well blow off his mom. That lady was no apron-wearing cream puff. She was an alpha female who commanded respect from her children, and it was willingly given. She might be tough, but she was loving and kind and fair. Her children adored her.

"Yes. She and dad want to meet you."

"You told them about me?"

Seeing the startled wonder in Rio's silver-gray eyes came as no surprise to Mick. He had a feeling his unassuming lover would react that way. "Of course." Unconcerned with his own nudity, he rose from the bed and sauntered over to stand in front of his mate. He bent to Rio and silently crowed when Rio obediently raised his chin to accept the kiss he bestowed. "You're family now."

"I am?"

"You are."

When Rio leaned into him and wrapped slim arms around Mick's waist, Mick knew he'd hit a nerve. He was almost sure he knew what thoughts were brewing in Rio's head, so he simply held the younger man and patiently waited. Standing there, he let their bodies sway back and forth a bit and rubbed his chin over Rio's soft, freshly washed hair. He breathed in the herbal scent of shampoo accompanied by Rio's distinctive and slightly sweet musk. The combined scents reminded him of the outdoors and he closed his eyes, content to linger here for as long as Rio needed to set his thoughts in order.

"Mick?"

"Mmm?"

"Will you go home with me?"

It was just as he'd thought. "You want to see your dad."

"Yeah."

"All right. I'll make plane and hotel reservations for us. Is a couple of days from now okay? Although you can resist shifting now when the moon rises, I think it would be best if you spend the next two nights getting better acquainted with your wolf."

"Yeah, that's fine. You know, I want to do this so bad but I'm..."

"Scared?"

"Yes."

"It's okay to be scared. I'll be there with you, and I really think you're doing the right thing. If for no other reason than to give your dad some closure."

"Yeah. Hey."

"What?"

"Did you ever notice how you sometimes finish my sentences?"

"I do?"

"Yes."

Mick wasn't sure what to think. He wasn't aware that he'd been doing it. "Should I apologize?"

"No. I just thought I'd mention it. I actually think it's kinda --"

"Cool?"

Rio laughed and stepped back. "Cut that out."

Mick grinned and reached out to ruffle his hair. "You need a haircut. This is longer than your wolf's coat."

"You gonna cut it for me?"

"Hell no! I'll take you to the place where I get mine cut. Let me get showered. We'll go out for breakfast then get your hair dealt with." A sudden thought struck Mick. "Hey, didn't you say your birthday was coming up soon?"

"Yeah."

"When is it exactly?"

"Today."

"Idiot. You weren't going to tell me, were you?"

"What for? It's no big deal."

"Not to you maybe, but later I get to smack your ass nineteen times." Seeing the outrage on Rio's face, Mick laughed and quickly added, "What would you like for a present? Pick something special. Something you really want."

Rio looked away and shuffled his feet. "I already got what I want. And he's taking me home."

Stunned by that bashful and softly voiced admission, Mick felt unexpected tears blur his vision. He was at a total loss and after a few frozen seconds, grabbed Rio, hoisted him up in a fireman's carry, and strode into the bathroom with him.

"Hey! What are you doing?!"

Without stopping, Mick went straight to the shower stall, entered, and turned on the taps. Three separate showerheads released a fine spray of clear warm water that resembled a hard summer rain. They were instantly soaked.

"What the fuck! I just got dressed!" Rio yelled.

Mick put him down and backed him up until Rio rested against the shower wall. "So now you'll get undressed. This is your fault. You don't get to say things like that without paying the consequences." With the shower water disguising his tears, Mick was able to look his young mate in the eyes.

Rio cocked his head and Mick could actually see understanding seep into the beautiful, luminous silver-gray orbs that were trained on him. His lover smiled and reached up to wrap wiry arms around his neck. "So what are the consequences?"

"I make love to you. Right here, right now."

Rio frowned a bit as though considering the idea; then in a teasing, resigned tone of voice gave in. "Okay."

Mick laughed but quickly sobered. Staring straight into Rio's eyes he said, "I love you." Rio glanced away and Mick could see him rapidly blinking his eyes. It seemed he wasn't going to be the only one struggling with tears.

When his gaze returned to Mick's, Rio answered, "I love you too…even if you are an alpha."

"How did you know I was an alpha?"

"You're too bossy to be anything else."

"Are you all right with that? I know you're not fond of alphas."

"I think I'm getting over that. Besides, you're my alpha, so it's okay."

Guided by the wash of tenderness that swept over him, Mick combed back strands of Rio's wet hair, ran his hand over the young man's jawline and with a finger under his chin, tilted his head up. His mate's mesmerizing eyes were shining and those tempting lips parted in an invitation not to be refused. When their mouths came together it was a sensation exquisite in its simplicity. Soft lips, warm breaths and the moist playground wherein two tongues tangled and teased.

Between hot kisses and intimate caresses, Mick peeled Rio out of his soaking clothes. Face-to-face, he let his hands slide over his smooth, wet skin. His fingers lingered on the tiny nubs of Rio's nipples, and he nearly groaned as they hardened when he toyed with them. Bending down, Mick took one in his mouth. Pinching it lightly between his teeth, he sucked and lashed his tongue over it to the sound of Rio's moans. When released, that little mound was rosy pink and swollen.

Mick repeated his actions on the other until they matched and with his free hand stroked Rio's straining cock, palmed his plump balls and teased the smooth skin that led to his tiny, twitching hole. Straightening, Mick cupped the cheeks of Rio's ass and hoisted him up. "Put your legs around my waist," he ordered. When Rio complied, Mick carried him to the nearest showerhead and twisted it so the water flow was directed away from them. He took Rio's hands and urged him to lift his arms. Guiding them upward, he curled Rio's palms over the stem of the showerhead. "Hold on tight and don't let go."

With Rio anchored both above and below, Mick again cupped the cheeks of his ass. He found Rio's tight little bud and eased inside the soft, wet heat with the middle finger of his right hand. When his finger slid easily in that lubricated sheath, Mick added a second finger then a third until he was rhythmically fucking and easing open the clasping ring of muscle that guarded Rio's entrance.

Rio was obviously enjoying the procedure. Bucking his hips, he was pushing into every inward slide of Mick's fluted digits while demanding, "More. Fuck me, *fuck me.*"

Taking his mate at his word, Mick withdrew his fingers, lined up his cock and pushed. He was in halfway before Rio's passage clamped down on him. "*Son of a bitch,*" Mick groaned, dropping his forehead against Rio's shoulder. "Not that I don't love the way your body just grabs me, but ease up a little, baby. I want all the way in. Come on now, let go." He raised his head and nuzzled Rio's throat, kissing and licking over his slick, water-dampened skin. Rocking his hips just a bit, Mick continued to cajole his lover. "Gonna let me in? Mmm?" Reaching between them, Mick found where they were joined and massaged the tightly stretched skin that encircled his cock. Rio gasped, arched, then relaxed back into Mick's hold, allowing his cock to slide all the way inside. "Oh yeah, that's it. *So fucking good.*"

*"Mmm, Mick."*

Rio's soft, passionate moans aroused him almost as much as the tight grip of his satiny sheath. Mick let his gaze wander over the sleek symmetry of his mate's body. Rio writhed so gracefully in his arms, his muscles stretching and flexing beneath the lustrous gleam of smooth, creamy skin. His slightly rounded pecs were accented by nipples now prominent and rosy. His taut abdomen contracted, the muscles rippling as he rolled his hips and arched his back in an effort to capture more of Mick's cock. His thighs were long and firm, his legs gripping Mick with a strength born of urgent desire. And his cock. So hard and full, its ivory length clearly showed the prominent, plump vein that enwrapped and fed it, bringing a rosy flush to the smooth crown. It lay against Rio's flat stomach and quivered with his every move.

That beautiful, angelic face wore a passionate, needy expression. His full lips were parted and those mesmerizing silver-gray eyes were closed, perhaps to better concentrate on the sensations Mick knew were coursing through his body. "Nnn, unhh, Mick...move, God, please move."

Ensorcelled by his mate's seductive form and openly sensual demands, Mick did as he was asked. His buttocks flexed as he ground in a bit before withdrawing. The velvet grip of Rio's passage massaged the full, hard length of his cock with each subsequent thrust. It was heaven, it was bliss, it was nirvana embodied in this one small package. The young man he held in his arms.

Every stroke of his cock within his lover's body sent the need rising higher. He raised his arms, cupped his hands over the top of the tiled shower wall, and pumped his hips, pounding into him with a hard, fast rhythm that had them both gasping for air. Rio cried out again and again, but they were cries of pleasure and so Mick continued driving them both to the brink. The hard knot of desire beneath his belly grew hotter and harder to contain. The pressure built, drawing his balls up as buzzing shocks coursed up his spine. After endless breathless moments of agonizing anticipation, the pleasure escalated into a wild eruption of sensation that burst between them along with the spurts of semen that spattered against Rio's skin and within the confines of his milking passage.

Mick felt as though his soul was being sucked into the hot depths of his mate and he willingly gave every bit of himself. Nothing mattered but this joining, each to the other, filling and being fulfilled. By slow increments their mutual climax diminished and with it Mick's power over his own body returned. He released his grip on the shower wall and, dragging in breath after breath, he wordlessly urged Rio's hands to release from the stem of the showerhead. Staggering back, he eased his legs down then turned him a bit and sat on the built-in tiled seat that occupied a recessed space on one of the walls. With Rio lying sprawled against him, he closed his eyes and listened to the soothing blend of falling water and the deep steady breaths of his spent lover.

A trickle of warmth tickled the inside of his thigh and Mick frowned until he realized what it was, and then a lazy smile curved his lips. "You're leaking, baby."

"Mmm?"

"My seed's dripping out."

"It's your fault. Filled me up."

"I guess I did. Happy birthday."

\* \* \*

Rio stared out the window from the passenger side of the rental car he and Mick had picked up at the airport several hours earlier. Before him was a sight that made him ache. It was the house where his life had begun. The place where he'd grown up with two loving parents. Only the death of one of them had allowed such misery to enter in the form of she, who in superficial appearance only, replaced his mother. Swamped by emotions, not the least of which was trepidation, he blindly reached for the hand of the man who sat next to him. His hand was taken in a firm, sure grip and that contact calmed the panic that threatened to send him running away once more.

Gaze on the front of that brick, ranch-style home, he took a deep breath. "I'd never be able to do this if you weren't with me. Thank you."

A reassuring squeeze came from the hand holding his. "You're welcome. Are you ready to go in?"

"No, but let's do it anyway."

"Your dad said he'd be alone, right?"

"Yeah. Just like I asked when I first contacted him."

Rio recalled that emotion-fraught phone call. Wanting to avoid his stepmother, he'd contacted his father at his office. After establishing his identity and getting through the initial incredulity his call had caused, Rio's father had broken down and cried. His reaction had caused Rio to lose it as well, and it was only Mick's intervention that had finally brought some semblance of intelligence to a conversation that was punctuated by nearly incoherent, tear-laden ramblings. Even now the thought of it caused a tightness behind Rio's eyes and he fought to keep his control.

Another squeeze brought Rio out of his reverie. "Come on, baby, you can do this."

Rio looked at his mate. Never had Mick looked so strong, solid, and dependable as he did at this moment, and never had Rio been more grateful for his presence. Nodding, he released Mick's hand and got out of the car. The two of them met on the sidewalk and traversed the length of the concrete walkway to the front door. Before he was able to knock, the door was flung open and Rio's father appeared.

There'd been some changes since the last time Rio had seen him. A few more wrinkles had appeared around his eyes and some gray was now shining among the glossy, light brown strands of his short hair. Rio wasn't sure, but he thought his dad looked thinner, leaner; but when those familiar arms reached out to him, none of that mattered. He rushed into them and again was the boy he'd been before he'd run away.

Just as when they'd first spoken on the phone, there were tears as they wordlessly held each other and cried. Rio's father was the first to recover and pulling away a bit, he wiped his eyes. "I told myself I wouldn't do that but seeing you again. I just...couldn't..." He paused to get hold of himself and tried a new tack. "Come in, come in." He ushered them into the living room. "I'm sorry." He held his hand out to Mick. "I guess you've already figured out that I'm Rio's father, James Hardin. You must be Mick."

"I am," Mick replied, shaking his hand. "I'm pleased to meet you and really, there's no need for apology. This can't be easy for you. Either of you."

Rio intercepted Mick's understanding look and gave him a tremulous smile.

"That's true. Please, sit down." The three of them took seats, he and Mick on the sofa with his father taking the wing chair across from them. James stared at him like a starving man eyeing pastries though a storefront window. "My God, you've grown. I have...so many questions, but I'm afraid to ask. I'm afraid I'll drive you away again, or that you'll get angry and leave."

Blinking back fresh tears, Rio fought to hold on to his composure. "You didn't drive me away."

"Then what did? *Why, son?* Why did you go? Why did you just disappear without a word?"

"I...oh God. I don't want to tell you this. I don't want to hurt you."

"You think your running away didn't hurt me? I've died inside a thousand times wondering where you were, wondering what happened to you!"

Rio felt his insides curdling with shame and guilt at the pain in his father's voice. Suppressing a sob, he managed to gasp, "I'm sorry. I'm so, so sorry." A strong arm looped itself over his shoulders and he leaned into the safety of Mick's embrace.

"Mr. Hardin, I appreciate how difficult this is, but I think we'll get through it a little better if we try and stay calm," Mick lightly admonished.

"You're right. You're perfectly right. I'm sorry. I'm sorry, Rio. I just..."

"No. Don't apologize," Rio told him, sitting up straight. He gave Mick a grateful look and nodded when Mick released him. "I have so much I need to tell you. Most of it you're going to hate, but it all has to start with why I left. If we can't get beyond that then nothing else will matter." He took a deep breath. "The reason I left was because --"

At that moment there was the sound of a door opening at the back of the house and the patter of small feet approached. A boy of about five years of age with strawberry blond hair and freckles came running into the room. "Dad! We're home."

Rio looked on in amazement as the child flung himself in his father's arms. "Who? Who's this?"

"This is Jack. He's been with us for about a year now. He was a foster child. Carol and I adopted him."

"Adopted?"

Horrified, Rio suddenly felt as though the air was being sucked out of the room. Black spots began dancing in front of his eyes. His imagination supplied him with a picture of this sweet child being abused by his stepmother just as he had been. Nearly to the point of passing out, his strained psyche took another hit as a waking nightmare walked into the room.

"So the prodigal son returns. Hello, Rio," Carol said, greeting him with a familiar smirk.

Stunned, Rio felt as though he were being torn in two. From a distance his human half heard his father ask Carol why she'd come home early. He listened to her reply of how Jack's playmate had gotten sick and so their play date and shopping had been cut short. His other half, the wolf, had awakened and was rising within him. The beast was angry, snarling and snapping at Rio's control. He wanted to be unleashed against this human who had caused them so much pain. Rio stood up.

"Dad?" he managed to ask, though his voice had gone husky and dropped an octave. "Can Jack go somewhere? We need to finish our talk."

His father turned a startled gaze on him. "Of course but, are your eyes…glowing?"

"Dad, *please.*"

His father sent the little boy off to go play in his room, and at the same time Mick rose up to stand beside him. "Control it, Rio."

Shaking his head, Rio suppressed the growl that burned in his chest. "It's too late. Just don't let me kill her."

"*What?*" Carol squeaked.

Rio ignored her and addressed his father as he fought to hold on to his wavering humanity. "A few weeks ago I was savaged, held prisoner, and used as a fuck toy by a lunatic who turned me into a werewolf. That's just one of the many wonderful things that have happened to me since I left here. You want to know why I ran away? Because of her. She seduced me and made me have sex with her. I was fourteen. I didn't know how to handle it. I didn't know how to stop it. When I told her I didn't want to do it, she said she'd tell you it was my idea and my fault. I was hurting you and it was killing me. That's why I left." Turning away from his father's shocked and disbelieving expression, Rio turned his gaze on the woman he'd spent the last four years hating. "Tell him."

Carol, her eyes wide with shock, but resolute nonetheless, shook her head. "I don't know what you're talking about."

As though giving his wolf permission, her words triggered Rio's shift. There was a scream and the next thing he knew he was standing over her cowering form. Carol had dropped to her knees and was crying and cringing away from the wolf that was snarling and growling at her from mere inches away. At that moment he wanted nothing more than to savage this sniveling, foul-smelling wretch of a human being, but his human side still held some sway and kept his primitive impulses leashed.

A voice sounded from behind him. Mick. "Lady, you better speak up and tell the truth. I'm supposed to keep him from killing you, but that doesn't mean I won't let him damage you a little. In my opinion you deserve it."

"No! Don't! All right! I admit it, it's true! Everything he said is true!"

With the truth finally revealed, Rio felt vindicated. For a moment a huge weight was lifted from his shoulders and he shook with elation...until he looked at his father. James Hardin had the appearance of a man whose entire world had been ripped apart. His eyes were dark pools of devastation in a face that had gone slack with shock. Seeing such emotional damage and knowing that he'd played a part in it made Rio sick. His elation turned to grief and the wolf, whimpering in distress, backed away from the woman who'd ruined their lives. The sound brought his father's gaze to rest on him.

There was no blame or heat in his voice when he spoke. "I don't know if you can understand me. I don't know what to say. I need time to think. I never thought I'd ask this of you, especially when you've come home after being gone for so long, but...please leave."

Nearly staggering under the crushing blow he'd been dealt, the wolf threw his head back and howled. That heartbreaking sound echoed from the walls with a soul-piercing reverberation. When the last of his sorrowful ululation died away Rio chanced one last look at his father. The man had lowered his head, and Rio could see tears spatter against the hands he had tightly gripped together in his lap. Unable to bear the thought of facing his father as a human, Rio turned away and on unsteady legs, wobbled to the front door and waited. A split second later Mick was there to open it, and with his mate, Rio once more left his childhood home behind.

The ride to the hotel was made in silence. Mick seemed to understand his need for isolation. Rio retained his wolf form until they reached the hotel where he transformed in the car, then followed Mick to their room. Exhausted and empty, he dropped facedown on the bed. He didn't protest or help when Mick removed his shoes and undressed him. Like a child, he was put to bed. The drapes were drawn and the television turned on with the sound down low. He felt the mattress give as Mick silently settled down beside him. With his eyes closed, Rio merely drifted for a time then escaped into sleep.

Rio awoke to quiet, true darkness and the knowledge that his father now more than likely hated him. The pain he'd been holding at bay crashed through the damaged shell of his heart, shattering that fragile organ into countless pieces. His gasping intake of breath caused the strong arms that held him to tighten, and Rio sought refuge in the comforting caresses and crooning growls of his mate while he sobbed out the absolute misery that engulfed him.

Since leaving home he'd dealt with so many things, so much emotional upheaval, but through it all the one thing that had kept him going was the knowledge that there was at least one person in the world who loved him. His father. Even though he now had Mick in his life, to have that essential relationship torn away was devastating.

Mick's voice, rough but gentle, murmured in his ear. "Shh, baby, it's all right. It's going to be all right."

"I should never...have come back," Rio hiccupped between teary sniffs while burrowing deeper into Mick's sheltering embrace.

"Yes, you should, and I'm proud of you that you did. Not only was it the right thing to do, but your intervention may just have saved that little boy the pain of what you went through. I just hope your dad has the good sense to believe the truth of what he was told."

"Why would he? He probably hates me now. Not only did I ruin his life, I'm a…a freak."

"Bullshit. It was damned obvious how much he loves you. And you listen to me. Being a werewolf doesn't mean you're a freak. Paranormals have been a part of this world from its inception. Just because there were more humans than any of the other species, they were allowed to believe for far too long that they were the only ones who had the right to openly exist. That's over, and it's been that way for years. If anyone's a freak, it's those who can't accept the differences of others. And another thing, you did not ruin your father's life." The strong arms that held him tightened and Rio was lightly shaken. "You did nothing but tell the truth, and that may be hard to live with, but it's a far better thing than allowing him to bury his head in the sand, especially if it means letting that bitch do as she pleases because he doesn't have the guts to deal with it. If he's anything like you, I believe your father will find the courage he needs to do what's right and when he does, you'll be hearing from him again."

"Yeah, he'll want to berate me in person for destroying everything that's important to him."

"Stop insisting you're the bad guy. Like it or not, you're one of the victims."

"Don't call me that. I'm not a victim." Rio squirmed away and sat up. Mick followed his example.

"No? Who was abused by his stepmother? Who had to leave his own home and turn to hustling to get by? Who ended up trapped and tormented by a sicko, perv werewolf?" Insistent fingers grasped his chin and he was forced to meet the steady, supportive gaze of his lover. "That was you, Rio. You. You're not the villain here. You've suffered more than anyone in this whole sorry mess. Don't try to take the blame. It's ludicrous, self-destructive, and unnecessary. You can resent the hell out of me for doing this, but I don't intend to let you get away with it. I understand your need to grieve and to purge these emotions, but once that's done it'll be a far more admirable thing for you to move forward with your life rather than to wallow in the mistaken belief that any of this is your fault."

"You...you can be a real bastard, you know that?"

"Yeah? What else is new?"

Still feeling tired but also somewhat relieved and at peace after having vented his grief, Rio thought for a moment then answered, "I'm hungry."

Mick enfolded him into an all-encompassing embrace and squeezed him tight. Rio grunted as his ribs creaked. "It's too late for room service, but I bet we can find an open pizza joint that'll deliver. Go blow your nose and wash your face."

Rio nodded and started to roll out of bed but was suddenly dragged back. Mick nuzzled his temple. "I love you. It *will* be all right, one way or another. Your dad's not the only one who needs time right now. Give yourself a break, Rio."

Blinking back the fresh tears that threatened to fall, Rio again nodded. "I love you too, and I will. Just keep reminding me."

"I will. I promise."

A gentle pat to the ass sent Rio on his way, and he heard Mick calling the front desk for a pizza delivery service recommendation as he walked into the bathroom. Turning on the light, he blinked and brought a hand up to his brow to shield his dazzled eyes. When he could see again, he found Kleenex and blew his nose then washed his face. Looking at himself in the mirror, he grimaced. Swollen eyelids and swollen lips. Great. His face was as pale as his newly shorn hair, and he dragged a hand over the bedraggled tresses.

Rio stared into his own eyes, but for the next few moments all he could see was a replay of the events from earlier in the day. Dropping his gaze from mirror, he took a deep breath. Mick was right. He and his father both needed time. This afternoon's incident would cause him pain for a very long time but he would endure, just as he'd endured everything else. At least now he didn't have to do it alone.

Taking comfort in that thought, Rio turned off the bathroom light then walked out to the other room and into the warm, loving arms that awaited him.

* * *

*Three months later...*

"The hot dogs are done! That's everything off the grill. You guys got the rest ready? I'm starving," Rio sang out as he walked in from outside through the kitchen doorway.

Two men turned toward him at his entrance. One was his mate and lover, and the other was essentially his brother-in-law. The resemblance between them was quite pronounced as they stood side by side, but in Rio's eyes there was no comparison. After setting the plate that held the hot dogs down on the counter, he wrapped his arms around Mick's waist and angled his head up for a kiss. It was freely given and he reveled in the thrill of sensation that shot through him every time this man touched him.

"All right. That's enough of the lovey-dovey crap. There's an innocent bystander here, you know. I shouldn't have to see this, especially when I'm between girlfriends," Jed groused.

Rio stepped back from Mick and grinned. "Did Sherry dump you?"

"Nobody dumps me, whelp," Jed growled, aiming a smack at Rio's ass.

Laughing, Rio jumped out of the way and hid behind Mick.

"You'd better teach your pup some manners, bro, or he's going to end up in trouble."

"Well, we can't have that. Not now after we've finally got him straightened out." He slung an arm over Rio's shoulders and drew him back around to face Jed. "Apologize, pup."

"*Mick*," Rio complained, surprised at his lover's stern order.

Mick leaned in and whispered in his ear. "Just give it your own special twist."

Understanding, Rio managed to keep his smile at bay and put on a contrite expression. "I'm sorry, Jed. Sorry that you can't manage to hold on to a woman." Mick's amused snicker triggered Rio's grin and the two of them watched as Jed first scowled then shook his head and chortled.

"Fuckers. Put those damn dogs in the oven with the rest of the meat, you little shit. Mom, Dad, and the others should be here any minute now."

Rio happily complied and when a knock sounded at the front door he was the first to call out, "I'll get it."

It was an exciting day for Rio. He'd been accepted to Indiana University and Mick's family was throwing a GED graduation/college acceptance cookout in his honor. Expecting to see Mick's parents or sister and her husband and family, Rio was totally stunned to find not only his father, but the little boy he'd been introduced to months before standing outside the door.

"Dad?" Rio managed by way of a greeting.

"Hello, son. May we come in?"

"Uhh…sure, please. What are you doing here?" His father was smiling, and Rio felt a seed of hope take root in his heart.

As his father and Jack entered by way of the front door, Mick and Jed appeared from out of the kitchen. Introductions were made and greetings exchanged and with that out of the way, James Hardin came straight to the point. "I need to talk to you, Rio. If you're willing to hear me out."

"Of course I am."

Jed came forward. "You all need some privacy. How about if Jack and I go outside? Jack, do you like swings?" The little boy nodded. "That's great. We've got a couple of doozies out by the garage. Come on, buddy."

Looking to his dad for the okay, Jack grinned when James nodded. The little boy took Jed's hand, and Rio noticed the long look that passed between his father and his mate's brother. A strange sensation shot through his middle but quickly disappeared when his dad cleared his throat.

"I'll join them, if you'd like," Mick volunteered. His offer caused Rio a moment of misgiving, but the offer was quickly turned down and he silently heaved a sigh of relief. Whatever it was his father had to say, Rio was sure he didn't want to hear it without Mick to back him up.

"No. You're Rio's… significant other." His dad grimaced. "I'm sorry. I don't know the proper term."

"That'll work," Mick answered with a smile.

"Thank you, but as such, this concerns you as well. As you both can imagine, things have been difficult over the last few months. I had so much to deal with but first of all, I want to…no…I need to apologize. Rio, son, I'm so sorry. I've failed you so miserably. I had no idea. I should have known --"

"No, Dad, don't, please. It wasn't your fault," Rio insisted, interrupting him. "As Mick has so patiently pointed out to me time and again, it wasn't my fault and it wasn't yours either. It was Carol." He paused; the name he spoke left a bad taste in his mouth, but he quickly went on. "She chose to take advantage of me. I should have told you, but shame and fear are tough opponents to take on when you're fourteen, and she knew that. What's done is done. We both made mistakes. Me for not telling you about what was going on and maybe you for not leaning on me a little harder until I spilled my guts." Rio looked to his mate and got an approving wink in return. He smiled. "I'd like to, more than anything, put this behind us."

James nodded. "I'd like that too. I've missed you so much. I want my son back."

His words released the restraint that stood between them, and father and son embraced each other. There were some tears this time but nothing like the flood that had been released when they were first reunited. When they drew apart, both were bashfully smiling.

"Why don't we sit down," Mick suggested. "I'm sure you have more to tell us."

With a deep sigh, James took a seat on the sofa. "That I do."

Mick sat in a nearby easy chair and Rio sat on the arm, appreciating the security of his mate's arm as it encircled his waist.

"Carol and I are divorcing. We came to an agreement. I gave her the house and she relinquished all claim to Jack."

"The *house?* Dad," Rio began, dismayed at the thought of that woman taking his childhood home.

"I know what you're thinking," James interrupted. "But it's okay. It's not the house that matters, it's the good memories we retain from the time we spent there. The time when your mother was alive and the three of us were happy. I didn't want to stay there anymore, Rio. Not after what happened; that's why I let it go so easily. Besides, I had to think of Jack. I couldn't let Carol retain any rights to him. I failed one son; I wasn't about to fail another."

"You didn't fail me," Rio insisted. "Stop saying that."

James gave him a melancholy look. "I just wish Carol could be prosecuted for what she did to you, but there's no evidence against her. I don't think the court would accept a werewolf-induced confession."

Rio gave him a shamefaced grimace. "Probably not."

"I might be able to help with that," Mick interjected. "What I can do may not be strictly legal, but I guarantee she won't go near another child for the rest of her life."

"Do it," James said without hesitation. "As long as it doesn't cause her physical harm," he specified albeit it seemed, with some reluctance.

"She may have a few nightmares, but there won't be a mark on her."

"Good."

"Damn," Rio softly cursed. "You guys are hard-core."

"Just practical," Mick gently corrected.

"Well, anyway," James said, changing the subject. "The good news is, with all that behind us, I've sold my practice and Jack and I are moving."

"Moving where?"

"Here. Good optometrists are needed anywhere. I've bought a house with an attached office space. I decided I wanted to be closer to my son. My oldest son," he amended with a grin.

Rio laughed with joy. "That's so cool! That's the best present I'll get today. If I get presents, that is."

Mick chuckled. "Whelp. You'll get presents. Guaranteed from my parents, though I'm not telling you what they got you."

"Presents?" James asked. "I know I missed your birthday. Are you celebrating today?"

"No. We're celebrating your son's admission to IU."

"Oh my God. Congratulations! I'm so proud of you!" James rose from his seat and Rio went to meet him. The two of them exchanged a hug. "When you have time, I want to hear about everything that's been happening since you left…if you feel up to sharing it with me," his father told him.

"Even the bad things?" Rio asked.

"Those too. They should be part of my burden as well as yours."

"Dad," Rio began.

"Hey," Mick interrupted. "Enough serious talk for today. I see my sister Natalie's here with Rich and their brood. Poor Jack's about to be overrun, though hopefully my nieces and nephews have enough manners not to be too hard on him."

"We should go," James said. "We're interrupting the celebration. I just wanted to let you know what's been going on." He turned to Rio. "And I wanted to tell you how much I love you and how happy I was…am that you came back. I really want to be a part of your life again. If you'll let me."

"Of course I will. I love you too, which is why you can't go," Rio told him with all the honesty and happiness he was feeling coloring every word. "This celebration is for family. How would it look if my dad leaves?"

"That's right," Mick added. "Stay, please. We want you to join us."

"Are you sure? I didn't bring anything."

"You brought yourself and Jack; that's more than enough."

James laughed. "All right, but you have to let me help out with something."

"Right now the only thing you can help with is the eating," Rio told him. "Later you can help me clean up."

"I'd be happy to."

"Good. Now that that's decided, come on outside. You can rescue Jack while I introduce you to my sister and her husband," Mick ordered with a grin.

At that moment, Mick's parents arrived. The yard became a mass of smiling adults and running children, but eventually they got everyone organized and settled down to eat at the picnic tables Mick had bought for the occasion. Everyone seemed to be getting along well. Rio watched his dad talk and laugh with Mick's family and it made him so happy he could burst. Jack too seemed to be having fun with Natalie's kids and he resolved to get to know his new little brother now that they'd be living close.

At one point Jed joined him as he was refilling his plate from the dishes on the food table. "I've been talking with your dad. He's nice."

"I think so," Rio replied.

"He seems awfully young to have a kid your age."

"He was twenty when I was born. My mom was actually three years older than him."

"Ah, that would explain it. He's cute too. I see where you get at least part of your looks, though his coloring's darker than yours."

Rio stared openmouthed at Jed.

Looking him straight in the eyes, Jed demanded, "What?"

"Uh, nothing. I just…I'm not sure what to say to that. You think my dad's cute?"

"Yeah. Is there anything wrong with that?"

"I guess not."

"Good. I've volunteered to help him move in and get settled. Remember when I told you if I found a guy as cute as you I might be willing to give the other side a try? Who knows. I might end up being your daddy as well as your brother-in-law." With a wicked wink and a grin, Jed sauntered off and plunked himself down on the picnic bench next to James. Staring after Jed in shock, Rio jumped when a voice spoke near his ear.

"You look like you've seen a ghost. Everything okay?"

"Jed likes my dad," Rio said, offering a dazed explanation to Mick, who was looking at him with concern.

Rio's words brought a relieved smile to his face. "Is that all? I thought it was something bad."

"*Mick.* This is my dad we're talking about. Besides, Jed said he might end up being my daddy. *My daddy, Mick. Do something!*"

Mick just laughed. "A double whammy. Listen, calm down, your dad can take care of himself and Jed won't do anything to force the issue. Despite the fact that he sometimes acts like a dog, he's an honorable one. Besides, if Jed's wolf says James is the one, well, nobody comes between a wolf and his mate. We both know that, don't we?"

"Yeah, but…"

"No buts. At least not here. Now later I'll handle any butts you want to throw at me." Mick cupped one firm cheek of Rio's behind.

"Ass," Rio replied.

"That too. Oh shit, I'm being given the evil eye over my disgraceful behavior. Give me a minute to grovel to my mom then come and save me."

Not caring who was watching, Rio threw his arms around Mick's neck and soundly kissed him. When they drew apart, Mick cocked an eyebrow and smiled. "You realize you're in trouble now too, don't you?"

"Then we'll just have to save each other, won't we?"

"I think we already did that."

"We did and since we've had practice, this should be a breeze."

Laughing, Mick took Rio's hand. As the two of them went to meet their fate, Rio knew that with this man by his side he could face anything. Even a temporarily disapproving alpha mother-in-law.

THE END

# Kate Steele

By day, mild-mannered Kate Steele lives the quiet life in rural Indiana with family in a century-old farm house. Ensconced in front of her trusty computer, she bravely fights off the attention of two annoying, yet sweet, lovebirds and two dogs who always seem to have to go outside. Transformed at night into a wild and fearless creature, Kate visits alien worlds, fights insatiable bloodlust, howls at the moon, and always brings home the most utterly gorgeous alpha male to indulge in wild sexual fantasies. Ah, the good life.

Visit Kate on the Web at www.katesteele.com.

# TITLES AVAILABLE In Print from Loose Id®

A GUARDIAN'S DESIRE

Mya

ALPHA

Treva Harte

CROSSING BORDERS

Z. A. Maxfield

DAUGHTERS OF TERRA:

THE TA'E'SHA CHRONICLES, BOOK ONE

Theolyn Boese

FAITH & FIDELITY

Tere Michaels

FORGOTTEN SONG

Ally Blue

HEAVEN SENT: HELL & PURGATORY

Jet Mykles

INTERSTELLAR SERVICE & DISCIPLINE:

VICTORIOUS STAR

Morgan Hawke

SLAVE BOY
Evangeline Anderson

SOMETHING MORE
Amanda Young

STRENGTH IN NUMBERS
Rachel Bo

THE ASSIGNMENT
Evangeline Anderson

THE BROKEN H
J. L. Langley

THE RIVALS: SETTLER'S MINE 1
Mechele Armstrong

THE TIN STAR
J. L. Langley

THEIR ONE AND ONLY
Trista Ann Michaels

*Publisher's Note: The print titles listed above were previously released in e-book format by Loose Id®.*